WOMAN

WOMAN

BY RICHARD MATHESON

GAUNTLET PUBLICATIONS

■ 2005 ■

Woman © 2005 by **Richard Matheson**
Jacket Art © 2005 by **Harry O. Morris**
Interior Page design by **Dara Campbell**

ISBN 1-887368-75-2

This book is a work of fiction. Names, characters, places and
incidents are either the products of the author's imagination or
are used fictitiously. Any resemblance to actual events or loca-
tions or persons, living or dead, is entirely coincidental.

Manufactured in the United States of America

FIRST EDITION

Gauntlet Publications
5307 Arroyo Street
Colorado Springs, CO 80922
United States of America
Phone: (719) 591-5566
email: info@gauntletpress.com
Website: www.gauntletpress.com

To the women and soon-to-be-women I have known in my life.

My loving mother.

My Aunts Evelyn and Lise and their daughters Vivian, Helen and Ethel.

My Sister Gladys and her daughters Doris, Karen and Janet.

My Sister-in-law Mary and her daughters Pat, Barbara, Maureen, Christine, Kathy and Geraldine.

My Sisters-in-law Pat and Andrea.

My Cousin Lily.

My Daughter Tina and her daughters Lise, Valerie and Emily.

My Daughter Ali and her daughter Mariel.

My Daughter-in-law Trish and her daughter Kate.

Sweet Diana.

And last but obviously not least, my wife Ruth Ann, the love of my life.

THURSDAY

STATION KBNY, 3:26 p.m. Dr. David Harper: *Candidly Speaking*. How may I help you?

I don't know if anyone can help me.

You sound bitter.

I *am* bitter.

What's the problem?

I am unable to suppress my total frustration at being a woman.

Is this regarding career or personal life?

I don't know any more. Both, I suppose. Certainly, my

career. The better I do at my job, the more I'm resented by the men. The only time they accept a woman is if she plays the game.

Which is—?

Subordination. Yes, sir. No, sir. Bleached hair—preferably blonde—tight clothes, lots of perfume. Willingness to flirt, to be "available."

I understand.

Except for the one woman executive in my department who doesn't have to do any of these things. The men accept her. (pause) As a *man*.

I see.

So I've just been wondering if I'm not wasting my time trying to be an uncorrupted woman.

Would you rather be a *corrupted* woman?

I'd rather be a *man*.

All right, let's just say, for a moment, that you could be a man. What would you do?

Use my *power*.

Against—?

I don't know.

Now you sound distressed.

I *am* distressed. (pause) Are we getting *anywhere*, Doctor?

Are women *really* progressing at all?

Well...I'm going to say something that may surprise some of my listeners—women in particular.

What's that?

I question whether the feminist movement is progressing.

For God's sake, *why*?

Because the very structure of society places distinct limits on women. Before they can be truly free, that structure has to be changed. It's not enough to give women fragments of rights within society as it now stands. The old, traditional superstition of "otherness" regarding women has got to be eliminated. They must first be recognized as *human beings*, then as females. Candidly speaking, what women need right now is their own personal Lincoln.

And if that Lincoln fails to appear?

I wonder.

4:47 P.M.

DAVID UNLOCKED the door and came into the apartment, carrying a large paper bag with several liquor bottles in it. Closing the door, he crossed to the livingroom bar and put down the bag. Taking out bottles of Chardonnay, Pinot Noir and a fifth of Scotch, he set them on the bar. Will it be enough? he thought.

Liz wouldn't think so.

But then she never did. Tonight, she could be right, though, with Charlie, Max and Val coming over. Well, there were more bottles under the bar. They'd manage. Anyway, they'd all be leaving early for the show.

Folding the paper bag, he carried it into the kitchen and put it in the pantry closet, glancing at the brown-edged hanging plants. We're not exactly green thumbers, he thought with a faint smile. There was a note on the kitchen

7

table. *Do we have enough wine, liquor and ice?* David shook his head, making a soft, amused sound. Yes, Liz, yes, he answered in his mind. Fear not.

Taking off his tweed jacket, he hung it over the back of one of the kitchen chairs, then folded back the cuffs of his shirt and loosened his tie and collar. Would he have to put on a fresh one? he thought, a different tie? He shook his head again, smiling. Stupid question, of course. Liz would expect him to wear his tuxedo tonight. After all, it *was* an awards show they were going to and Liz was up for an Emmy. Oh, yeah, he thought. The tux would be mandatory.

There was another note scotch-taped to the refrigerator door. *Don't forget to take the ordurves* (Liz was never very good at spelling) *out of the freezer.* Opening the freezer door, David took out the tray of hors d'oevres and placed it on the counter. Too soon to microwave? Probably.

Closing the freezer door, he glanced toward the window as the wind picked up outside. It had been cold and gusting all day, threatening rain. Hope it does, he thought. This is what the weather's supposed to be this time of year. Not like last years heat spell in March.

He was opening a large can of cashew nuts when the doorbell rang. Now who the hell could that be? he wondered. Charlie was always an early arriver but even he couldn't be here this soon.

Putting down the can of nuts, David left the kitchen and walked across the living room to open the door.

A young woman was standing there, wearing a simple yellow dress and a light jacket. She was about twenty, David estimated. "Yes?" he said.

Her voice was soft, timid. "Doctor Harper?" she asked.

"Yes?" he said again.

"My name is Ganine Woodbury." She pronounced her first name as though it was spelled Jeanine.

"*Yes?*" he said. Who was she and why was she here? he wondered.

"I live on the seventh floor," she told him.

"You do?"

"Yes," she nodded. "I saw the name on your mailbox and wondered if—"

He waited. "*If—*" he said then.

"You were—" He saw her swallow nervously. "I asked the doorman and he said you were." She hesitated, then added quickly. "Doctor Harper of the radio show, I mean."

He tried not to show how uncomfortable he felt. "What is it you want?" he asked.

"I listen to your show all the time," she said. "You help so many people."

He had to cut this short, he knew. Liz would be back soon. "Miss—" he started. He'd already forgotten her last name.

"Woodbury," she said, "Ganine Woodbury."

He nodded, "Yes," he said. "I'm rather busy at the moment, Ms. Woodbury." He assumed she was unmarried.

"*Could you help me?*" she asked, in a pained voice.

For a moment, he was speechless. Then, hastily, he said, "I don't have a practice anymore, Miss Woodbury."

"Call me Ganine," she said, her tone almost pathetic.

He grimaced. "Miss Woodbury, I don't have a thera-pist–patient practice any longer. It's strictly books and the radio program."

"You write *books*?" she said in surprise. "I didn't know that."

"Yes, well—" he began.

"*You're the only one who can help me,*" she broke in, sounding frightened. "The only one who knows what it's like."

Now he felt as perplexed as impatient. "I don't—" he started.

"*What it's like to be a woman,*" she explained.

He felt sorry for her now. Still— "*Look*, Ganine I'd like to be able to help you but my wife and I are having a group of friends over very shortly and—"

"*Can I come?*" she blurted.

He was speechless again.

"*Please?*" she said.

"I'm sorry, that's impossible," he told her. "And now you'll have to excuse me. I have to shower, change my clothes, prepare for—"

"*Please help me*, Doctor Harper." She was pleading now.

"Ganine—"

There were tears rising in her eyes. "*Something terrible is happening to me*," she said.

He stared at her, not knowing what to say.

"I don't know what it is but I can feel it growing every day," she told him in a breaking voice. "I can feel it getting worse and worse every day."

He had to end this, that was clear to him. "Look, I'll tell you what I can do," he said. "I'll give you the name of an excellent therapist. I'll make a phone call—"

"*No!*" She cut him off so sharply that it made him start. "I need *your* help," she insisted. "You're the only one—"

"*That isn't true*," he interrupted firmly. "The therapist I'm going to recommend is highly qualified. She's been in practice—"

"*A woman?*" she said; she sounded repulsed. "*That wouldn't work.*"

"*Ganine—*"

"I don't *want* her! I want *you!*" She sounded like a petulant child now.

"*I don't have a practice any longer*," he said, "You must understand—"

"*I don't know who I am anymore*," she said as though he hadn't spoken. "I look at my face in the mirror and I can't—"

She broke off, glancing to the side as footsteps approached in the corridor. In a few moments, Liz Harper appeared, carrying tied together bakery boxes and her purse. She gave Ganine a look of cold curiosity as she brushed by her and entered the apartment. David stepped aside to let her pass. "Hi," he murmured.

"We don't have much time, David," she told him.

"I know," he nodded. "Miss Woodbury was—"

He broke off as Liz headed for the kitchen where she put the bakery boxes and purse on the table and turned on the oven.

"Look, Ganine," David said. "I really can't talk to you now." He started to turn. "Let me get you the name of a—"

"*Can I see you tomorrow?*" she interrupted.

He turned back, struggling to sound patient; she was clearly very disturbed. "I can't help you personally," he told her. "All I can do is recommend—"

Again, she interrupted. "But you help so *many* people," she said in a pained voice.

"On the *radio*, Ganine," he said. "Not—"

"David, *there isn't much time.*" Liz's voice was curt.

"All right," he answered. "I'll put the name and telephone number of this therapist in your mailbox tomorrow morning," he told Ganine.

Her voice was trembling now. "*Please help me, Doctor Harper,*" she pleaded.

"Ganine, I'm not unsympathetic." he said, "I simply can't—"

He stopped, hearing the rapid click of Liz's high heels as she crossed the living room floor. Looking around, he saw how rigid her expression was.

She pushed by David. "I'm sorry but my husband can't talk to you right now," she told Ganine, "you'll have to excuse us."

David winced as she closed the door in Ganine's face, then turned back toward the kitchen, gesturing as though to tell him: *See how simple it is.*

"She was terribly disturbed, Liz." There was an edge of disapproval in his voice.

"Aren't we all," she said coldly. "Are you sure we have enough ice?"

David looked at her, frowning.

"Well, *do* we?" she demanded.

"Yes, Liz, *yes.*"

Ignoring the bite in his tone, Liz started toward the bedroom. "I'm going to take a shower and get dressed for tonight," she told him. "Will you make sure to put that tray of hors d'ouvres in the oven when it's hot enough. Not the microwave, the *oven*," she added.

He nodded, "I will."

"*Thank* you," she said, moving toward the bedroom. Abruptly, she turned and moved to the bar. Returning to the kitchen, David stopped to watch her opening the door under the bar and taking out a bottle of white wine and a bottle of Vodka. "I hope to hell we have enough," she said.

"We're not going to be here that *long*, Liz," he answered. "And we'll probably be doing our heavy drinking at the banquet."

"We're still going to need—*Oh!*" She had stopped moving suddenly, pressing her right hand against her forehead.

"What's wrong?" he asked. He moved toward her in concern.

"My *head*," she said, teeth clenching in a pained grimace.

"A headache?" he asked.

"What else?" she said tensely. She hissed, eyes closing.

"It just hit you?" he asked sympathetically.

"Yes, David, *yes*. It just hit me. No, that's not exactly right. It's been threatening all day." She pressed both hands to her head. "God *damn* it! On today of all days."

"Maybe it'll let up if you take a pain pill," David suggested. "You have some, don't you?"

"Oh...*shit*," she said, infuriated.

Taking down her hands, she started toward the bedroom again, her expression taut and angry.

"Maybe you should—" he began.

"*Cancel*, sure. That's a *great* idea." she snapped.

"I was going to say maybe you should lie down for a while—"

"There isn't *time* David," she told him in a tense voice, "Just get those goddamn appetizers in the oven," she added as she walked into the bedroom.

"Right." he said.

He stood in the livingroom without moving. Perfect timing, he thought. Well, it was not that much of a surprise. Liz's headaches had been more and more frequent since she'd become the producer of *Country Boy*. Stress, he thought. The number one cause of headaches in the world? Most likely. Maybe the cause of most ailments in modern society. And Liz was a woman in a man's world. The age-old problem. Where was that Lincoln? Somewhere in the wings, he hoped. Or else there'd be a lot more headaches for a lot more women for a lot more time.

He started into the bedroom to take his tuxedo out of its garment bag. He assumed it would still fit. It had been a long time since he'd worn it.

5:59 P.M.

David came out of the bedroom, wearing his tuxedo trousers, his white, studded shirt and bow tie, black socks and patent leather shoes. He carried his jacket which he hung in the entry closet. He'd put it on later.

He turned on all the lamps and glanced around the living room. Neat enough, he told himself. Liz wouldn't think so but then she never did. She kept saying they should move to a more spacious apartment. Especially, now, considering her position as the producer of a top-ranked sitcom at NBC.

"You'd better make sure those appetizers come out all right," he heard her calling from the dressing room. Where she is doubtless working toward perfecting her award-winning appearance, he thought with a smile. "I will," he called back.

"They may need another few minutes in the oven."

"Why didn't we just microwave them?" he asked. "A lot simpler than—"

"*They come out better in the oven*," she cut him off.

"Yes, ma'am," he muttered.

"Did you *hear* me?" she asked, her tone aggravated.

"I heard," he answered.

"Then *answer*."

"Yes' ma'am, lady producer," he said.

"Ha. Ha," she said. "Make sure the ice bucket is full."

He nodded. "*Right*." The ice bucket was full. "Ice is fine!" he called.

"Good." she said.

"How's your headache?" he asked, heading for the kitchen.

"Not a hell of a lot better." Her voice was tight.

"I'm sorry," he said.

"So am I," she answered.

"Did you take a Darvocet?"

"Half of one," she told him. "I can hardly afford to fall asleep at the show."

"No," he muttered.

"*What*?" she asked.

"I said, no, you can't afford to fall asleep at the show."

"That's all I'd need," she said.

He went into the kitchen and opened the oven door. The heat was on the warm setting. Reaching into the oven he picked up one of the crab-stuffed cakes and put it in his mouth, making puffing noises at the heat of it. He chewed it then. Good, he thought.

"They're *fine*!" he called.

"Well, take them out of the oven then!" she said impatiently.

God, I hope you win the goddamn Emmy tonight, he thought. It's going to be a miserable weekend if you don't.

He put on an oven mitt and lifted out the pan of hors d'ouvres, setting them on the counter.

He was starting to transfer them to a serving platter when the doorbell rang.

"*Oh*, yeah," Liz said in the dressing room, "You can bet your life that's Charlie. Always the first. What time is it?"

"A few minutes past six," he answered. "You want me to let him in?"

14

"Unless you want *me* to let him in wearing my brassiere and panties."

"I'm sure he wouldn't mind," he said to himself.

"What did you say?" she asked

"Nothing," he answered, walking toward the door. The doorbell rang again. "*Anybody home?*" he heard Charlie's muffled voice in the corridor. "On my way," David murmured.

He reacted with abrupt surprise as he opened the door.

Standing next to Charlie was Ganine. Still wearing the same dress and jacket.

Charlie thrust out his beefy right hand. "Doctor! How ya doin'?" he said, his tone loud and hearty. He was a heavy-set man in his fifties with a bushy bandit's mustache, a flushed complexion.

Charlie made a courtly ushering gesture to her, "After you, my dear," he said.

David knew that he should tell Ganine she wasn't coming in, that she'd have to leave. Before he could act though, she entered with a timid smile, glancing worriedly at David.

"Met this lovely little lady on your doorstep," Charlie said. He pointed at Ganine. "Ganine?" he said. "Jeanine," she corrected. "Ah," said Charlie. He grinned at David. "Must be from your side of the tracks."

David couldn't decide whether or not to close the door. If he closed it, it would be as much as inviting Ganine to stay. If he left it open—

"Delighted you're going to be with us," Charlie told Ganine, patting her back affectionately. "Touch of youth. We can use it." He beamed at her, then chuckled. "Doubly delighted for that matter. For once, I'm not the first to arrive. Dreadful habit."

"Ganine isn't—" David started, then broke off as Charlie took a step into the living room. "Where's that Emmy-winning producer of mine?!" he called.

Liz answered from the dressing room. "Will you stop it?" she scolded.

David stepped in close to speak to Ganine. "I'm sorry but this—"

"I know I shouldn't do it," she said.

"No such animal!" Charlie was booming. "We all win tonight! It's in the bag!"

"Have a drink, Charlie," Liz called.

"You twisted my arm," he answered, starting for the bar.

"Ganine, this is really out of the question," David told her sternly.

"I won't get in anyone's way," she said.

"That isn't the point." His voice rose uncontrollably. "We simply—"

"Are the hors d'oevres out yet, David?" Liz called.

"Almost!" he called back. Jesus, he thought, if Liz saw Ganine here again—inside the apartment. The notion made his teeth clench.

"Well, get them out!" Liz told him.

"All right!" David looked tensely at Ganine. "Ganine, *please*—go," he said. Groaning softly, he moved toward the kitchen. I shouldn't be doing this he thought, I should be getting her out of here.

"What's your pleasure, my dear?" Charlie asked. Oh, no, David thought.

"Uh...nothing," Ganine told him. "Thank you."

"Oh, come on," Charlie said. "Festive occasion. Have to imbibe."

"Just...juice then," Ganine said.

"Only juice?" Charlie said disapprovingly. "Come on. A little wine maybe?"

"Who are you talking to?" Liz asked from the dressing room.

To hell with the hors d'oevres, David thought, turning back abruptly. The girl had to go.

"Just your pretty little guest," Charlie called.

Dead silence. David felt his stomach muscles pulling in. "Okay, just juice," Charlie said. "I find that questionable though."

David was approaching Ganine when Liz came in wearing her dark red evening gown, her hair held up by combs. When she saw Ganine, she stopped abruptly, staring at her with angry incredulity.

"Need more orange juice here," Charlie told her.

"*David.*" Liz's voice was tight as she gestured toward the kitchen with her head. "Oh, God," he whispered, moving behind her.

"So what do you do for a living, Ganine?" Charlie asked. "Model?"

David didn't hear her answer as he followed Liz into the kitchen.

"*What in the holy hell is going on?*" she demanded.

"Look, I—" David started.

"*Did you invite her in?*"

"No, of *course* I didn't," he answered sharply. "*Charlie* brought her in."

"*Charlie?*" she glared at him. "*That* makes sense?"

"*Liz.* When I opened the door, she was standing beside him and obviously he thought she was invited too," he began to explain in a carefully controlled voice.

"Well, *get her out of here*," she interrupted. From the look on her face he could see that she still had the headache or a large portion of it.

"I'll try," he said.

"What do you mean, you'll *try?*"

"Liz, *take it easy will you?*" he said, beginning to lose patience.

"*Take it easy?*" she said, "The most important night of my career, a splitting headache, this...*flake* crashes our party and you tell me to take it *easy?*"

"She's *disturbed*, Liz. There seems to be something seriously wrong with her."

"*I'm* disturbed too. Are you planning to offer her *therapy?*"

"Oh, for Christ's sake," he said irritably. "I didn't *plan* on this, you know."

"All right, all right, I'm sorry," she said. "Just…please get her out of here."

He squeezed her hand. "I will," he reassured her.

Liz turned to the counter to finish placing the crab-filled cakes on the platter. Earlier, she had removed a selection of miniature cookies from one of the bakery boxes and arranged them on another platter. Holding out that platter, she told David to put it on the living room coffee table. "And a bottle of orange juice for Charlie," she added.

"Yeah," he said distractedly, wondering how he was going to get Ganine to leave without making a scene. Opening the refrigerator, he took out the half gallon bottle of orange juice, shut the refrigerator door and picked up the cookie platter.

"Get her out of here," Liz said quietly, her back still turned to him. David raised a glance toward heaven, then started into the living room.

As he entered he saw Charlie filing an ice-cube filled glass with Scotch. Charlie was a heavy drinker, eventually turning raucous. Not tonight, dear Lord, David thought. To his added distress, he saw that Ganine was sitting on one of the easy chairs, a half-filled glass of orange juice in her right hand.

"Ah, more juice," Charlie said, taking the bottle from David. "A little more, my dear?" he asked Ganine.

"No, thank you," she said, smiling timidly.

"All *right*." Charlie gave her a broad smile and plopped himself down on the sofa. He made a toasting gesture with his glass of Scotch. "To you," he said, "You *should* be a model, you're that lovely."

Ganine replied softly. "Thank you."

"Just the God's truth," Charlie told her.

"I need to speak to you, Ganine," David said. She looked at him fearfully. "In the kitchen," he told her.

Her uneasy hesitation made Charlie look at David curiously. "Something wrong here?" he asked.

"No, no." David told him, "I just need to talk to her for a moment."

"Can't do it here?" Charlie asked.

"No." David's tone was curt. "In the kitchen, Ganine."

She stood as Liz came into the room, her face pale, an hors d'oevres-bearing wraith. "Good evening Mrs. Harper," Ganine said.

"Well, aren't you the beauty?" Charlie said. "Hey—I take that back. You look terrible," Charlie said in concern. "Are you sick?"

Liz shook her head, putting down the platter of crab-filled appetizers. Ganine started toward the kitchen, followed by David.

"What's going on?" Charlie asked.

"She's not our guest," Liz told him, making no effort to keep her voice down. "She just showed up at our—oh, my *God!*" she threw her head back with a gasp of agony.

"What *is* it?" Charlie asked, sounding frightened.

"My *head. It's going to explode.*" Liz was barely able to speak.

David started out of the kitchen, his face distended by fear. "*Liz,*" he said.

"A headache *tonight?*" Charlie said. He sounded almost displeased. "Have you taken anything?"

She didn't answer, groaning weakly, both hands to her head.

"Liz, you'd better cancel—" David started.

"No! I *can't,*" Liz broke in with a cracking voice. "I have to—!"

Suddenly, she stopped, a blank expression on her face.

"What *is* it, Liz?" David asked.

"Liz come on, *say something,*" Charlie said.

She touched round her head with shaking fingers.

"*What?*" David asked.

She swallowed dryly. "Gone," she muttered.

"What do you mean?" David looked confused.

Unexpectedly, Liz uttered a short, barking laugh. "It's

gone," she said, her tone incredulous.

"Well I'll be goddamed," Charlie said. He took a long swallow of scotch. "I've heard of psychosomatic but this is ridiculous."

Liz laughed again. There were tears in her eyes. "Thank God," she said, "Thank God."

David moved to her and sat beside her, putting an arm around her shoulders. "This is…what? Remarkable."

"*Incredible*," she said.

"At least," Charlie said. He took another long drink, sighed.

David looked at Ganine. She was standing motionless in the kitchen doorway looking at Liz. Well, he thought abruptly, still that problem. "I'll talk to her now," he murmured to Liz.

"Yes," she said. She sounded weak.

Standing, David took hold of Ganine's arm and guided her into the kitchen.

"I'm glad your wife is all right," she said. "That didn't need to happen."

The remark passed over him. "Listen. Ganine," he said gently. "You really have to go."

"But I won't bother anyone," she said, "I'll just sit quietly. I just want to be near you."

"Ganine, this is a very important evening for my wife. It disturbs her—"

"But she's *all right* now." She cut him off.

"Ganine, that's really not the point—"

He broke off as Ganine suddenly pressed both hands over her face and began to cry, her back and shoulders hitching with sobs. "*Ganine*," he said, "There isn't any need to—"

He stopped as she tried to speak but couldn't, crying harder. Oh, God, he thought. This is a bloody nightmare.

"It's all right, Ganine. Just—"

He started, tensing, as she pressed against him abruptly. He glanced at the living room. Liz was sitting on the sofa, looking at him, her expression undecipherable. Anger? Confusion? Uneasiness? All of them in combination?

"What is she, *crying*?" he heard Charlie say.

"Yes." Liz's voice was strangely unconcerned. The sudden, miraculous disappearance of her headache seemed to have momentarily drained her of determination.

"You know, I bet it was neuralgia," Charlie said, "Doesn't that come and go?"

Liz shook her head. "I don't know."

"Well, anyway, it's bloody marvelous. It would be damned tragic for you to miss this night."

"Yes."

David found himself patting Ganine's back awkwardly. "I really think you need to see this woman therapist," he said.

"No," she whimpered. "*No. Please.*"

He looked at Liz with a hapless expression as she came into the kitchen.

Now what am I supposed to do? he wanted to say.

Liz started to speak when the doorbell rang, then looked at David, her expression as hapless as his. Her reaction surprised him. Where was the resentment now? Liz made a faint sound of—was it possible?—surrender and turning, left the kitchen. David took out his handkerchief and handed it to Ganine. "Stay here," he said. "I'll be back in a few moments." Well, what the hell else can I do? he asked himself. Drag her to the front door and pitch her bodily into the hallway? Sure.

Leaving the kitchen, he saw Max and Barbara Silver entering the living room. Liz kissed Barbara on the cheek, welcoming her.

"Are you all right?" Barbara asked, "You look a little peaked."

"I'm sure I do," Liz said. "I feel all right though." She gave Max a peck on the cheek. "Max," she said. Over at the sofa, Charlie called out, "Hello, people!" Liz helped Barbara off with her shawl. Max, tall, grey-haired and bearded, waved to David as he approached them.

"You look lovely," Liz said to Barbara.

"Thank you, sweetheart." Barbara smiled.

"What about me?" Max said, "Do I look lovely?"

"You were born lovely," Liz said, straight-faced.

"That's what they tell me," Max replied. There was little love lost between them.

Charlie came over and gave Barbara a bear hug. "Barbara, my adored one," he said. He looked at Max. "Hello, Mr. Head Writer," he said.

"Mr. Exec Producer," Max returned.

"Nervous abut tonight?" Barbara asked Liz.

"Only enough to come out of my skin," Liz answered.

"Think how Val must feel," Barbara said.

"I'd rather not," Liz told her.

Max looked over toward the kitchen and saw Ganine standing in the doorway. She'd dried her tears with David's handkerchief and looked under control again.

Max looked at Charlie. "Something we should know about?" he asked. Charlie was noted for the number of young women he dated and bedded.

"Stranger in town," Charlie said.

"Uh-huh." Max looked at the glass in Charlie's hand. "What are you drinking?" he asked.

"Scotch. On the rocks."

"Embalming fluid," Max responded.

"That's right, you're a gin man aren't you? Shades of Gatsby."

"Also good for open wounds," Max said, starting for the bar. Liz took Barbara aside to talk to her. David wondered what to do about Ganine. The front door was available. He could physically push her out. That was impossible though. He was wondering now just how mentally disturbed she actually was. It was certainly a dilemma, no doubt of that. Which, none-the-less, left him nowhere. And Liz seemed to have deserted him now, leaving the problem entirely in his lap. *Well, you're the psychologist.* She'd said that more than once and would probably say it again.

22

At the bar, Max and Charlie were still razzing each other as Charlie re-filled his glass with Scotch.

"Gin will rot your brain, Max," he said.

"More than Scotch?" Max said. "No, scratch that. More than writing sitcoms?"

"Got a point there, Senor Silver," Charlie agreed.

"Max, would you pour me a glass of white wine over ice?" Barbara asked from across the room.

"Do it yourself," Max said.

"Well, aren't you the perfect gentleman?" Charlie said. "Allow me, my dear," he said to Barbara, "Not your fault you married a boor."

"Thank you, Charlie," Barbara said.

"My pleasure." He poured the wine for Barbara, adding ice to the glass. As he brought it to her, he looked at Ganine. "You all right, darling?" he asked. She smiled and nodded once.

David came over to Liz and Barbara. "Would you excuse us for a few moments?" he asked Barbara.

"Sure," she said. "I'll go flirt with Charlie. He doesn't think I'm shit."

"*Barbara...*" Liz looked at her accusingly.

"It's nothing," Barbara said, "I'm used to it."

She walked over to the sofa and sat beside Charlie. "Does this mean we're engaged?" he asked.

"No, just potential lovers," Barbara said, loud enough for Max to hear. He raised his martini toastingly, a scornful smile on his thin lips.

David took Liz to a far corner of the room.

"What?" she asked

He hesitated.

"*What*, David?" she said.

He braced himself, "I think it would be simpler to let her stay," he told her.

She looked astounded. "You have got to be kidding."

"Trying to put her out in her frame of mind could be more trouble than it's worth."

"David, I am not going to—"

"We're only going to be here for a little while," he said. "Just ignore her. She won't make a scene or anything and, when we leave, that's the end of it."

She stared at him, unable to speak.

"I really don't see any other way to go about it," he said, "Not without casting a pall over the entire evening."

Liz shook her head slowly. "I don't like it, David. I don't like it at all."

"Your headache is gone, isn't it?" he said abruptly.

"What has *that* got to do with it?" she asked, frowning.

"When it hit you a few hours ago…" He didn't know how to say it. "Had a headache ever come on that fast before?"

She looked at him questioningly. "I told you it'd been threatening all day."

"And has a headache ever become completely agonizing in a split-second?" he asked.

She stared at him, then, finally, spoke. "You're not trying to say—" she couldn't finish, the concept so unbelievable to her.

"I don't know, Liz." She saw that he was deadly serious though, and the smile that was starting to raise the ends of her lips disappeared. "There's something very odd about her. I'm going to get her to Dr. Wilson as soon as I can. She—"

"You actually think she had something to do with—?"

Again, she couldn't finish.

"Just think about it, Liz," he said. "There *are* people in the world with unusual abilities. I've even met one or two. I'm not saying this girl is one of them. But do you want to risk this night denying that she is?"

She said no more. Her expression one of flabbergasted disbelief tinged with an involuntary uneasiness. After almost a minute of silence, she walked away from him without another word.

"Well, come sitten-zee down, sweetheart," Charlie was saying to Ganine.

Moving to the bar, Liz avoided looking at Ganine as Ganine moved to one of the chairs and sat on it diffidently.

"This is Barbara and Max Silver," Charlie told her. "She's a nice lady, he's a Jewish Nazi."

"And he's an executive producer," Max said, "One step above the amoeba."

"Are you a friend of the Harpers?" Barbara asked. At the bar, Liz shot a glaring look at Ganine, then looked accusingly at David as he came up beside her. "Well, now she is here," she muttered.

"It'll only be for a little while," he promised.

"It'll be too long whatever it is," she said. Angrily she poured several inches of vodka into a glass, then added ice and tonic water.

"Your headache is gone," he said, "Just be grateful for that."

She did not respond but he could see that she was still uncertain about what he'd just suggested to her.

He poured himself the same drink as Liz's and they returned to the group. David sat, Liz chose to remain standing.

"So how are you feeling, Liz?" Charlie asked. "Internal whim-whams?"

"I'm all right," she answered quietly.

"Well, we should all clean up tonight," Charlie said. "Except for Max, he doesn't deserve it of course."

"And fuck you too," Max said.

"How are *you* feeling, Charlie?" David asked, trying to lighten the moment.

"About the awards, fine," Charlie told him. "About waiting until ten or eleven to eat, *extremely* dubious. That's why I've already eaten. Five o'clock is steak time to me." He winked at Ganine. "Right?"

She murmured something. "What, sweetheart?" he asked, cupping his right ear.

"I never eat meat," she repeated.

"Oh, now, that is un-American," Charlie said, grinning,

"What are you, a vegetarian?"

She shook her head, "No, I just don't like animals being killed."

"Charlie thinks that's what they're raised for," Max said to her.

"I prefer fish or chicken," David said, trying again to generate some amiability in the group. "With some attention to mercury levels, of course."

"You wouldn't say that if you tasted a nice thick slab of my barbecued steak, blood-rare preferred," Charlie told him. "Not to mention venison or wild pig."

"You *hunt*?" Ganine said. She looked distressed.

"With the best of them, my dear," Charlie told her. "Nothing to compare with it."

"Except for machine gunning a barrel of fish," Max said.

"Has anybody spoken to my brother since yesterday?" Liz changed the subject.

"I did," Charlie told her. "He'll be here."

"Alone?" Liz asked.

Charlie snickered, "Is he ever?"

"Not that anyone ever noticed," Max said.

David looked at Ganine. She still looked upset by what Charlie had said. He considered saying something about it, then decided against it. The less Ganine was involved in the conversation, the better for Liz, he decided. He wondered if he'd made a mistake telling Liz that he thought it was best to let Ganine remain. He wasn't at all sure about what he'd suggested to Liz about Ganine. Still, the almost uncanny onset, then abrupt cessation of Liz's headache couldn't help but give him pause.

He noted, with relief, that Liz and Barbara were talking about the awards in generally positive terms.

Ganine chilled the atmosphere again as she said to Liz, "Your plants look sick, Mrs. Harper."

Liz looked at her without expression, started to say something, then decided not to. "I'm not quite ready yet," she said. "If you'll excuse me." She started toward the bedroom.

"Care for some company?" Barbara asked.

"Sure, come on." Liz managed a smile.

Barbara stood and followed Liz into the bedroom.

"I'm sorry," Ganine said to Liz. Liz ignored her.

"We, uh, had a woman who took care of the plants," David said to Ganine. "She moved away though and we haven't found a replacement."

"I could take care of them for you," Ganine replied.

David smiled awkwardly. "Well..." he said, not sure how to reply.

"I love plants," Ganine said.

"Not Charlie," Max said, "He hunts them."

Charlie made a scornful sound, ignoring Max's remark. "All this...*dreck* about—"

"Euphemism for *shit*?" Max said with a thin smile.

"All right. *Shit* then," Charlie said, looking at Max with a cold expression. "All this *shit* about plants and trees and dying species. *Jesus Christ*, it's still a great big world out there. You ever drive across the country?" he asked Ganine. "*Space*, girl. Nothing but space." He looked aggravated, his cheeks reddening.

Max blew out a breath, obviously bored. "Heard some of your program this afternoon while I was driving home," he said to David.

Charlie gave Max a contemptuous look but went along with Max's changing of the subject, "Missed it myself," he said. "My ex-wife used to listen to you all the time though."

"That's what saved their marriage," Max said.

"Up yours, Maxie," Charlie said.

"As a matter of fact I agree with you, Doc," Max told him.

"On what?" David asked.

"On the failure of women's lib," Max answered.

***

Later that night, Liz told him about her conversation with Barbara.

"Who is this *girl?*" was the first thing Barbara asked.

"I'm goddamned if I know," Liz answered. "David said that she just showed up at the door when Charlie arrived and Charlie assumed she was a guest and took her in with him."

"That's weird," Barbara said.

"You want to hear *weird?*" Liz told her. "David thinks she might have had something to do with my headache."

"You had a headache?"

"A *whopper,*" Liz said. "It was in the works all day but it hit me like a ton of bricks. Just after I'd shut the door in the girl's face. I didn't tell you that she was at the door talking with David when I got home about five o'clock."

"I don't—" Barbara stated.

"The headache really hit me when I put her out. And, later, when I was talking to Charlie while David was in the kitchen with the girl—"

She broke off, a look of indecisive concern on her face.

"*What?*" Barbara asked.

"*Suddenly, I thought my head was going to explode,*" Liz said.

Barbara stared at her. "*Explode?*"

"Explode," Liz nodded. "I felt as though I was going to die. Then…" She grimaced, wishing she didn't have to go on.

"What? Then what?" Barbara asked anxiously.

"It all went away. *Boom.* Like that. *Gone.*"

"And you think—?" Barbara couldn't finish.

"I don't know *what* to think," Liz said, "But I…feel… uncertain about the girl. David said we should just let her stay until we left for the show. I *hate* the idea but…I'm just—" She gestured haplessly.

"Jesus God," Barbara said quietly. "This is really bizarre."

"Well, anyway, I have to let her stay. I'm afraid not to."

"Christ, I don't blame you." Barbara made a pained

look. "You think she…has some kind of *power*?"

"*I don't know*, Babs," Liz said, "I'll just be glad when we all leave for the theatre. I wish Val would get here so we can get out of here."

"Yes," Barbara nodded, then whistled softly. "I agree."

She watched Liz finishing with her make-up and putting on her earrings. "Well, let's forget it for now," Liz told her. "There's enough angst going on with the awards."

"That's for sure," Barbara agreed.

"How are things with you and Max? Still bad?" Liz asked.

"Still bad," Barbara said, "We haven't made love for a year." She made a scornful sound, "Made love," she said. "We never did. We fucked occasionally."

"I'm sorry, Babs." Liz patted her arm.

"Oh, it's not so bad," Barbara said. "I don't even miss it now."

"Well, you should," Liz said firmly. "You should get a divorce or, at least, get a lover."

"I dunno," Barbara shrugged. "It just doesn't seem to matter anymore."

"Well, *don't say that*. They demand sex when they want it or get it elsewhere. Why shouldn't we do the same?"

"I suppose," Barbara said. She heard Max's voice rise in scornful volume in the living room. "There he goes again," she said.

***

"The failure is that of society, Max," David said.

"Oh, bullshit," Max said. "Facts are facts. It's still a man's world. It works better that way."

"It doesn't seem to be working too well at all," David said.

"Well, it'd be worse if women ran the show. Let's face it, they *are* the inferior sex."

"Are they, Max?" David said. "They live longer. Resist stress better. Adapt to the environment better. It's really not a man's world at all anymore. The women are right up there with us. Or—maybe psychologically, 'somewhere above us'," he clucked. "Not that it does them that much good."

"I don't agree with you at all, Doc," Max said.

Charlie pushed to his feet."I need more Scotch," he said, moving toward the bar.

"Maybe we should all freshen our drinks," David said, "I feel a debate coming on." He stood and followed Charlie. "You have enough to drink?" he asked Ganine.

She smiled and nodded, a vague expression on her face. He wondered what her reaction was to what he and Max had just been talking about.

"Yeah, bring the gin bottle over here," Max said. "And a thimbleful of Vermouth."

Nothing was said as Charlie refilled his glass and David added tonic water to his drink. "You're not going to give credence to that asshole, are you?" Charlie murmured. David smiled.

They had just re-seated themselves when Liz and Barbara came in. Liz made a point of not looking at Ganine, unwilling to confront whatever irritation plus uneasiness she felt.

"We were just discussing your hubby's program this afternoon," Max said.

"Oh?" Liz looked mildly interested. "What was it about?"

"Oh, some pathetic broad was bitching about how miserable she was being a woman."

"And—?" Liz had tensed slightly.

"*And*—your hubby told her that he thought women's lib was failing."

Liz looked at David in displeased surprise. "You said *that*?"

"Well, not exactly. What I said was—"

"It isn't *failing*," Liz cut him off. "It's getting more successful all the time. That's obvious."

"I wish I could believe that," David said.

She looked amazed. "How can you *say* such a thing?" she challenged.

"Because I think there's been very little attempt by men to make contact with the feminine...*essence*, if you will."

"*So what?*" she said, "That's *their* problem, not ours. We're not in bondage anymore, that's all that matters. I know *I'm* not."

"I'm glad you feel that way," David said.

"No, I know what David means," Barbara said, "In a very real way, we're still segregated."

"*Segregated? How?*" Liz asked.

"Well, look what happens when we're born," Barbara said, "Right away, it's pink blankets and blue blankets. We aren't just babies. Already, we're sexes."

Liz started to argue but Barbara wouldn't let her. "We never have our own names. Our maiden name is the name of our father. Our married name is the name of our husband."

"What's the difference?" Liz said. "You think freedom means unisex blankets and your maiden name? There's a lot more to living, Babs. Anyway, I'm still Liz Kramer in enough places—like my bank account."

Barbara nodded, choosing not to contest Liz. She looked at David. "What do *you* think?" she asked.

"Well—" He wasn't sure he wanted to get involved in this discussion with Liz; it was more than a touchy subject to her. "The woman I was speaking to this afternoon on my program maintained that the one woman in her place of business the men accepted, they accepted only as a man."

"That's really irrelevant, David," Liz said, "Who cares how they accept her? She's in, isn't she?"

"True," he said, nodding. They were into it after all, he thought. Not for too long, he hoped. Still, he felt compelled to add, "There *is* a danger though of the female essence being jeopardized by being forced to—"

"Again with your 'female essence' crap," Liz interrupted. "What is it anyway? An idea *men* came up with. There are no substantial differences between the sexes—"

"But there *are*," Ganine broke in, looking upset. Liz threw an angry glance at her, then—visibly, David thought —retreated, still not certain about what David had suggested about Ganine.

The others had glanced at Ganine as well, clearly none of them having the least idea why she was there.

"It's environment," Liz finished, despite her uncertainty, not willing to surrender her point of view. "You know that better than anyone, David."

Only David noticed Ganine murmuring apologetically. "I'm sorry."

"I'm not sure," David said. He wanted the discussion to end. If only Val would arrive and he could suggest an immediate departure for the Emmy show, ending the uncomfortable presence of Ganine.

"That's the attitude that keeps the war between the sexes raging," Liz said. Didn't she want the discussion to end too? he thought. Or was it just stubborn resistance to deferring to Ganine being there?

Max made it worse by saying, cheerfully, "Maybe this'll be a fun evening after all." Liz looked at him coldly. Her producer-head writer relationship with Max was far from cordial.

Liz started to speak when the doorbell rang. "Oh, good," David said, quickly. "Now we can get an early start."

"On *what*?" Max challenged.

"On getting to the theatre."

"I most *definitely* cast a yea vote on that," Charlie said.

"I presume that's my baby brother," Liz was saying as she moved for the door. "Anyone need a re-fill?" David asked, Max drained his glass and held it out. "Gin and ice, bartender," he ordered, "breath of Vermouth."

"Right away," David glanced around. "Anyone else while I'm at the bar?" Barbara and Charlie shook their heads.

Liz opened the door. Val Bettinger (he'd changed his

last name for the show) gave Liz a wide smile. "Ta-da!" he said. "The star has arrived!"

"And we are orgasmically thrilled," Max said. He looked at Val's date, a show girl named Candace Regina wearing a leopard fur jacket over her low-cut evening gown. Val wore a white dinner jacket despite the weather. "So give us a hug, big sister," he said. She put her arms around him and he pressed his lower body hard against her. "Bon whatever the fucking word for evening is," he said. "Are we late?"

"As always," Liz said, smiling affectionately.

"Now, now," he chided. "Mustn't gibe an Emmy winner." His shiny black hair was primed into a lavish pompadour.

"You haven't won it yet, brother dear," Liz said, closing the door.

"In the bag," Val told her.

"We haven't met," Liz said, extending her hand to Val's date.

"She's my latest cunt," Val said, "Name's Candy Vagina."

"Now stop that," Liz said, not too critically. She smiled at Candy. "I'm Liz Harper and I'm not responsible for anything my brother says."

"My first name is Candy," Candy explained seriously. "*Candace* actually, but my last name is *Regina*," she added as though Liz had really believed her brother's insulting last name.

"You can see how I got it wrong," Val said.

Liz smiled at Candy. "Nice fur," she said.

"Val bought it for me," Candy said.

"Services rendered," Val said.

Liz scowled mockingly at him. "Take your jacket?" she asked.

"Sure," Candy said. She removed the jacket, revealing more of her very low-cut evening gown. Val made a leering face at her half-uncovered breasts. "Intellectual services, of course," he said. Liz groaned, "Come on in," she said.

The three of them started across the room, Liz carrying Candy's jacket. "Greetings, peasants," Val said.

"I'd bow but I'm sitting down," Max told him. Val snickered. Ganine made a faint sound, staring at the jacket. "Be a good girl and maybe you'll get one some day," Max told her.

"I don't want one," Ganine said, making a face. Liz carried the jacket into the bedroom.

"How you doin', Babs? Charlie?" Val said. Barbara said hello, Charlie made a slight gesture of welcome.

"Say hello to the people, Candy." Val told her.

"Hello," she murmured.

"Talking's not her specialty," Val said. Imitating Groucho Marx, he added. "Later on I'll tell you what is." He looked at Ganine in pleased surprise. "Good Christ, a *new face?*" he said. "And who are you, young charmer?"

"My name is Ganine," she said.

"Ganine Woodbury, Val," David said, returning with Max's drink.

"Indeed," Val said. He leaned over her. "I'm sorry, I'm already stuck with a date," he said, "otherwise, I'd make a move."

"*Val,*" Candy tried, in vain, to sound disapproving.

"And how are you, Doc Harper?" Val asked, "How's the network shrink?" His voice became high-pitched and tremulous. "Doctor Harper, sir, I'm having trouble getting it up. What do you advise?"

"Use it less, young man," David said, as though answering a genuine call.

"I *am*," said Val protestingly, "I've got it down to ten times a night."

David smiled and shook his head, extending his right hand to Candy. "I'm David Harper," he said.

"Hi," she answered.

"Is that a real leopard jacket you have?" he asked, glancing at Liz as she came back from the bedroom and went over to the bar to make herself a fresh drink.

"Uh-huh," Candy answered.

"Ex-leopard jacket," Max said. David smiled.

"Hey, Charlie," Val said, "we gonna sweep tonight?"

"Why not?" Charlie answered, almost apathetically.

"Well, control your enthusiasm—from the program of the same name," Val said.

"Usually nap time after dinner," Charlie said, taking a sip of his Scotch. He went back to his conversation with Barbara.

"Would you like a drink?" David asked Candy.

"Can you make a Margarita?" she asked.

"Can he make a Margarita?" Val said, attempting an Italian accent. "He's a doctori. He can-a make-a any woman he wants."

Candy looked confused, "Huh?"

"Forget it," Val said.

"I'm afraid I don't know how to make a Margarita, Candy," David told her.

"Oh. Well...Uh..."

David waited for her decision as Val walked over to the bar and put an arm around Liz's waist. "How you doin', Sexy?" he said.

"I'm okay," she told him.

"Nervous about tonight?"

"A little."

"Don't give it another thought. We don't win, I'll blow up the fucking theatre. *Country Boy* rides home a winner tonight."

He glanced over at Ganine who was looking at him curiously.

"Our show," he told her. "You've seen it, of course. Wednesday night, eight to eight-thirty?"

She looked blank, shook her head. Val murmured to Liz, "This is your *guest*?"

Liz gave him a Medusa smile. "David will explain," she said.

Val scowled, turning to face Ganine. "You really don't know *Country Boy*? Top ten? Thirty-seven share?"

She made a hapless gesture.

Val turned back to Liz. "The girl's retarded, I presume," he said.

The smile remained. "Possibly," she said.

"Who brought her here?"

"*No one*," Liz said tightly. "David said she was in the corridor with Charlie and Charlie thought she was a guest."

"She's not though?"

"*Hardly*," she said.

"When are we leaving?" he changed the subject.

She gritted her teeth. "As soon as possible," she said.

"Doesn't sound as though you're too crazy about her," Val said.

Liz was about to reply when David came over to them. "So what does Miz Einstein want?" Val asked.

"Gin," he said.

"No kidding," Val said, impressed.

"And Coke."

Val's lips puffed out as he laughed.

"That's her," he said. He looked at Candy as she approached the bar. Liz turned away, walking to the sofa to sit beside Barbara.

"Yeah, Candy is a connoisseur of booze all right," Val said, pouring himself vodka over ice cubes.

"What's that?" Candy asked.

"It means you have big tits," he told her.

Candy struck feebly at the space between them. "Don't say that," she said.

"Why? You don't have big tits?"

She frowned, "It's not polite to—"

"Hey, I didn't know that," Val interrupted in a mockingly sincere voice. "All these years I've been talking about big tits and I never realized. God *damn*."

He whistled softly, wincing as Candy punched him on

the arm. "*Ooh*," he said, "I love strong women. Don't you, Doc?"

David didn't answer, smiling as he handed Candy her drink. "Thank you, sir," she said, "I see that you're a gentleman."

"And *I'm not*?" Val said looking pained. "You cut me to the cock, dear girl."

Candy made a disapproving sound, starting toward the group, David and Val following. As she looked for a spot to sit, Max patted his lap, an exaggerated leer on his face.

"Don't trust him," Val told her. "He writes."

"Why did you ask me if my leopard fur was real?" Candy asked David. "Didn't you think it was?"

David didn't know what to say. "Doc-a-doc was zinging you without you knowing it," Val told her, "which isn't difficult, of course."

"*Zinging* me?" Candy asked, looking confused.

"Zing went the zip of my fly," Val sang briefly, seeing her still blank expression, he added. "Leopard? Fur? Endangered feces?"

"Feces?" she asked.

"Oh, shit," Val said, "you explain it, Doc."

"It's nothing," David said to Candy.

"But it *is*," Ganine broke in. Everyone looked at her with varying reactions from mild surprise to criticism. The room grew momentarily silent as Candy wedged herself down on Charlie's right side, filling the sofa and David and Val took chairs.

Charlie had an angry expression on his face. "For Christ's sake," he snarled. "What's the difference if some lousy, fucking cats die out?" Barbara, Liz and David looked at him in surprise.

"Amen," Val said. "Kudos, Charlie. Who needs leopards anyway? Well, Candy does. Right, Sugar Pussy?"

"Oh, stop," Candy said, looking embarrassed.

"So what the hell are we talking about?" Val asked, "Emmys or endangered species?"

"*Emmys*," Liz said sharply, glancing at Ganine with a frown.

"Right!" Val said. He looked excited suddenly. "Forget to tell you, Liz," he went on, "I'm working with some of the writers on a segment where I get to go dramatic."

"Oh, shit, here we go again," Max said, casting his gaze heavenward.

"Fuck you. What do you know?" Val said. "You're only the head writer. You give head but can't write shit." He looked at Liz. "Like this," he said. "Country Boy gets caught up with a traveling Shakespeare company and the lady director gets the hots for him and teaches him how to do Hamlet's soliloquy."

"*What?*" Max muttered with a pained expression.

Val ignored him. "She tells Country Boy it doesn't matter if the fucking words were written in the Stone-Ages—"

"Middle-ages," Max corrected.

Val waved away his objection, looking irritated, "Hamlet's just some ordinary cocker deciding whether or not to screw his mother, kill his uncle or blow his fucking brains out."

"Never heard Shakespeare explained so well," Max said. Val gave him the finger as David glanced at Ganine to see what her reaction was to all this. She looked perplexed, he saw. No wonder, he thought, God, let's just all get out of here.

"What'd you think, Sis?" Val asked.

She looked dubious. "Well," she said.

"It'll work, it'll work," Val told her. "Wait till you hear it." He took a big swallow of his drink.

"Let's get back to woman's lib before he decides to do King Lear," Max said.

"Who the hell is he?" Val asked, sounding aggravated.

"Some blind cocker," Max told him. "Man versus woman, folks? It was just getting interesting."

"What are you *talking* about?" Val demanded.

"Woman's Lib," Liz told him.

"Oh, shit, who wants to talk about that?" Val said.

"Doc Harper thinks it's going down the toilet," Charlie said.

"No shit." Val sounded interested now.

"What do *you* think, Val?" David asked. "What should woman's position be?"

"Oh, on her stomach definitely," Val said. He pointed at Candy. "Candy likes it that way," he added, leering at her. "Don't you?"

"*Val,*" David said. As Val looked at him, David looked toward Ganine. Val shrugged.

"In other words, women should be exclusively sex objects, right, Val?" Max said, goading him obviously.

"Not in other words, Maxie boy," Val came back. "Them's the words. Sex objects, *period.* I mean *except* for their period." He held out his glass, chanting, "*Wha-wha,*" in burlesque style.

"Val, be serious," Liz told him. Her tone was more affectionate than serious, though, David noted.

"Why, aren't *you* a sex object, Liz?" he said. As she gave him a mildly critical look, he added, "You are to me."

Liz groaned softly. "God," she murmured.

Val looked at Candy with an innocent expression. "Aren't *you* a sex object, Candy?" he asked, his tone making it obvious that he already knew she was.

"*No,*" Candy whined. "I have a brain too, you know."

Val looked astonished. "*I* didn't know that," he said.

"I doubt if you know it about *any* woman," Barbara said coldly. Everyone looked at her, surprised.

"*Ooh,*" Val said as though stung. "Right in the kishkes. Better keep an eye on her, Max." He turned to Ganine. "What do you think, sweetheart? I thought you were retarded because you never heard of *Country Boy* but I didn't *really* think you were. What do *you* think about all this?"

"I don't know anything about it," she said, blushing

slightly.

"Holy shit, she *is* retarded." Val looked around the group. "It's very simple, folks. Pay attention now. Men have cocks and women want them."

Liz looked incredulously at her brother. "*Penis envy?*" she said. "You can't be serious, Val."

"Am I *ever* serious?" he asked. Abruptly, he did look serious. "You *bet* I'm serious."

"Well, that's *ridiculous*," Barbara said. David had always suspected that Barbara didn't like Val but he'd never known it for certain until now.

Val pointed at Barbara but looked at Max. "Better watch her, Max," he warned.

"Not to defend my dear wife but Freud didn't think it was ridiculous," Max told him.

"Good ol' Ziggie," Val said.

Barbara's words overlapped his, "Freud was a goddamn chauvinist," she said.

Val assumed an over-ripe German accent. "Got'n'himmel," he said. "I thought he was a fucking Viennese."

"Val, come on. Be serious. I mean *really!*" Liz told him, "Why in God's name should women want that...damned *protuberance?*" she finished.

"Pro-*tub*erance?" Val said. "*Hoo-ee!*"

"I think men have vagina envy," Barbara said.

"*Pussy* envy?" Val said. "No way! I don't *want* one. I just wanna be *inside* one. With my protuberance, of *course*. Or—" He made a rapid tongue-lapping face at Candy who struck at the air in front of him again.

"You know," Max said, his tone gentle as though he was about to make a reasonable point. "The Hebrews have a daily prayer which goes—" His voice turned icy as he finished "—*I thank thee, Lord, for not having created me a woman.*"

"Yes. And Freud was a Jew," Barbara countered.

Val looked pseudo-startled at Max. "You married an

40

anti-Semite?" he said as though the notion shocked him.

"That's right!" Barbara exploded, causing everyone to look at her in surprise. "The ultimate goddamn defense!" she raged. "Call women prejudiced who've been prejudiced against since the beginning of time!" David was the only one who noticed that Ganine had silently applauded.

"Ooh, this is getting *good* now," Val said, grinning. "I can see why you wanted to get back to this," he told Max.

"Barbara is right in a way," David said, wondering immediately if this was going to delay their departure for too long a period.

"How's that, *Doctor*?" Max asked in a cold voice.

"Well," David said, "Freud's major theory was that man is incomplete. He meant, literally, *man*. He never thought of women as incomplete. Merely inferior."

"*Inferior*?" Barbara said angrily.

"Wait a minute, wait a minute." Val broke in. "We have an expert here. Let's pay attention. Okay, Doc. Enlighten us. What's the story about men and women?"

David smiled, knowing the reaction his answer would bring. "Men are afraid of them," he said.

"Afraid!" Val cried, looking amazed.

"That's bullshit," Max said.

"*Max*," Barbara said.

"Well, it is," he said.

Charlie pushed to his feet. "Speaking of shit," he said, heading for the bathroom.

"Let's hear what Doctori has to say," Val said. He did his Groucho impression again. "As crazy as it is."

David's smile was uncomfortable. "Maybe we should talk about this in the limo." He checked his watch. "It should be here any moment now."

"No, you've brought this up," Liz told him.

"I know but do we really want to go into this right now?"

"You're *on*, Doctor Harper," Liz told him only half in humor.

David blew out breath. "Okay," he said then.

"Let's have it," Max said.

"All right," David said, "The reason women have always been an oppressed minority is that men regard them as a menace."

"There I'm *with* ya, Doc," Max told him. "They *are* a menace."

"Put 'em away!" Val cried, "chain 'em to the wall!" He made a suggestive face. "Naked, of course," he added.

David ignored him. "This so-called 'alien' quality has always outweighed women's desirabilities."

"All three of them, including hands," Val said. "Or in Candy's case, four."

"Shut up, Val," Liz told him casually.

Val imitated Butterfly McQueen. "Yaz'm, Miz Scarlett! Yaz'm!"

"Go on, David," Barbara said, "I like what you're saying. Mostly."

"You would," Max said.

"All right. Brace yourselves, Max and Val," David continued. "Historically men have always been afraid of falling under the power of women and becoming slaves to them."

"Oh, Jesus Christ," Max muttered.

"*Ah*, yes," Val said, imitating W.C. Fields, "The old S and M syndrome. Know it well."

"Val, *shut-up*," Liz said.

Val looked hurt. "Talking like that to the *star*," he moaned.

"Let David speak," Barbara told him irritably.

"Christ, they're *all* turning on me," Val said. "Boo hoo times two. Okay—" his voice went guttural. "*Speak, Doctor Harper. Speak.*"

"Do we really want to—?" David started.

"*Yes*. We *do*," Liz said. David wondered what she was thinking.

He sighed. "All right," he said. "This traditional fear of

women has engendered a hostility which lurks behind a façade of domination. A façade which, hopefully, intends — as Esther Harding put it — to overcome her (meaning woman) — with a stroke."

Val again, as W.C. Fields, "Stroke me a stroke as fast as you can." He turned to Ganine. "You haven't said a word," he told her. "What do you think of all this?"

"I think Doctor Harper is always right," she answered.

David saw how Liz stiffened at Ganine's reply. Don't say anything to her, he thought with a sense of sudden alarm. He really didn't know if what he'd said about Ganine was nonsense or something to really be concerned about. He only knew that this was not the moment to test it.

"So what about *you*, Liz?" Val asked. "We already know that Babs agrees with the Doc, Candy doesn't have the slightest idea what he's talking about."

"I *do* so," Candy pouted.

"Yeah, yeah," Val said. "Liz? You agree?"

"More or less," she said.

"How much more and how much less?" Val asked.

"Why don't we just let David continue?" Barbara told him stiffly.

Val raised both arms, bowed to her twice in mock-abnegation, making East Indian chanting sounds of humility.

"Go on, David," Liz said. He had the feeling she was inviting him to say something she could disagree with.

"I don't like doing this on an evening when—" he began.

"Go *on*, David," She interrupted.

"Please, David," Barbara said.

"Let's hear more," Max told him.

"The mandate of the people," Val said. "Vox populi. Ducks copulate."

"Oh, I really don't—" David started uncomfortably.

"Where does all this fear come from?" Barbara broke in. "All this hostility?"

David exhaled wearily. No help for it, he thought.

"Well," he said, "In the beginning, from jealousy. Of woman's ability to give birth. Her ability to menstruate."

"That's one ability I could do without," Liz said, her features tensing.

"Amen," Barbara agreed.

Val started singing to Candy with the tune of "Putting On The Ritz." "Puttin' on the rag, do-ah, do-ah, do-ah."

"Val. *Enough*," Liz said.

Val hung his head in mock sorrow, sobbing quietly. David noticed how uncomfortable Ganine looked. He considered suggesting to her, that perhaps she'd rather leave than stay.

"*Go on*, David," Barbara said, almost ordering him.

"Very well," David conceded. "Because of this jealousy, man isolated birth and menstruation with taboos and rituals designed to handicap women. They couldn't approach food. Couldn't approach weapons, animals. And, of course, couldn't eat with their husbands, couldn't socialize with them. In some cases, couldn't even speak their husband's names aloud. Or any male relative's names."

Val's voice went falsetto. "Me bleed, og," he said answering with a guttural tone. "You goddamn shut mouth, woman!"

Liz gave her brother a weary look and spoke. "Then the double standard is based entirely on men's fear of women," she said.

David gestured in agreement.

"They know we can out-perform them sexually so they've handed us this crap about it being acceptable for men to fool around but not women. What men *really* fear about feminism is woman's demand for sexual freedom."

Val looked at her with a contrived expression of lust. "I don't fear it," he told her, "I just wanna get in on it." He bared his teeth in a maniacal grin. "How about a little incest, kid? Always did wanna get you in the sack. Well, not when I was eight. Though come to think of it—"

"Will you please *stop*?" Liz asked him, still more affec-

44

tionately chiding than critical.

"Don't knock it if you haven't tried it," Val said. He looked at Candy. "Tell everyone about your Uncle Waldo, sweetie."

Candy looked genuinely uncomfortable. "Val, please," she murmured.

"*David?*" Barbara said in a tight voice. "Ignore the idiot and keep on talking."

"Well, now, dearie, keep in mind that hubby is the head scribe on the *Country Boy* and I'm the star with *power*," Val finished in a threatening voice.

Barbara closed her eyes as though to shut away the sight of him. "Doctor *Harper?*" she said.

David was about to cut it all off, stand and insist that they leave. Instead, he went on speaking. "While it's true that men have always been afraid that women wouldn't be faithful to them, being natural born polygamists, they projected their feelings onto women. According to Proverbs —"

"My favorite book," Val said.

"' —the mouth of the womb' is never satisfied," David finished, ignoring Val.

"How about a little mouth-to-mouth resuscitation?" Val said to Candy.

Liz paid no attention to him, saying, "I'll tell you what the problem is. Men have always felt their potency threatened by women."

Val postured like a queen on his chair. "Well, that's a lot of poo-poo," he said archly.

Liz pointed at him, smiling thinly. "*Right on*, brother dear," she told him. "You think it's a joke but it's the truth. The increase in homosexuality is taking place because men are fleeing women. Fleeing masculinity."

"Who can blame them?" Max said with a thin, scornful smile.

"Thinking of joining them, Max?" Barbara said. He directed an arctic look at her.

David noticed how uneasy Ganine was. "Maybe we should stop this," he said.

Liz had noticed his look at Ganine. "*The rest of us are interested, David,*" she said.

"I know but—" David started.

"You were *saying*, Max?" Barbara said in a cold, demanding tone. My God, David thought, I never knew the two of them were so completely alienated.

"I was *saying*," Max responded in a tone equally cold, "who can blame men for turning queer? Women aren't women anymore. They're female men."

"So why shouldn't men become male women, is that it?" Liz asked him.

"That's it, Producer Lady," Max answered.

"If that's the exchange you want," Liz said.

"It seems to be the one *you* want," he replied.

"Balls said the Queen. If I had them I'd be King," Val broke in.

Liz smiled at her brother. Not affectionately now. "That idea doesn't bother me either."

"Liz, I know you don't believe that," David said, torn by ambivalence. On one hand, he wanted all of them to leave for the awards. (No matter how tense the limo ride might be). On the other hand, he couldn't just desert the discussion at this point.

"If I have to grow balls to make it in the 'man's' world, I'll do it," Liz said.

Max's smile at her was victorious. "You wouldn't be a women then," he said.

"I'd still have *won*," Liz told him.

The smile broadened on Max's lips. "I think De Sade said it best."

"You would," Barbara said.

"Whip them asses!" Val contributed.

Max ignored them both. "Woman is a miserable creature," he said "always inferior to man, less ingenious, less wise, a creature sick three-quarters of her life, sour of dis-position, cross-grained, imperious, a tyrant if you give her leave and base and groveling in captivity but always nasty, always dangerous."

"*Hallelujah!*" Val crowed with revival meeting fervor.

"What did you do, spend the last year memorizing that?" Barbara said, scowling.

"No, it just stayed in my memory, it's so convincing." He cut her off as she started to speak. "How about a shorter quote then? Richard Burton. 'They should be *abolished.*'"

Val cackled. "Full moon! Crazy time!"

"I think we're going into this little too deeply," David said.

But Max was on a roll now. "Or as Schopenhauer put it: Most men fall in love with a pretty face and find themselves bound for life to a hateful stranger, alternating—"

"Well, now we know who your real target is," Barbara said, trying to disguise the hurt in her voice.

David raised his hands. "*Folks,*" he said. "This is sup-posed to be a fun evening in case you forgot."

Max went on as though David hadn't spoken. "Consider the tyranny of the non-working wife," he said. "I don't know who I'm quoting now."

"Your*self?*" Barbara said icily.

"Maybe," Max responded. "The point is this. The non-working wife seeks status by driving her husband to higher and higher success and, if he fails, she treats him with con-tempt and withdraws all sexual reward."

"*Who* withdraws it?" Barbara snapped.

David sighed. Will we ever make that limo ride? he thought. It seemed less and less likely.

"This is great!" Val enthused, "I love it!"

"In case you're not aware of it, Max," Liz told him. "In the Western world, women are more than a third of the working force."

"*And the rest of them work at home,*" Barbara said.

Max laughed scornfully. "My ass," he replied. "Houses

47

and apartments are so filled with hired help and labor-saving devices, women never have to lift a goddamn finger." Again, he cut off Barbara as she began to speak. "If there ever was an Atlantis, it undoubtedly sank from the weight of household appliances."

Val cackled again, then, hissing, clutched at his groin. "Hate to miss a word of this," he told them, "but I have to take a leak."

He moved to the bathroom and knocked on the closed door. "Almost finished, Charlie?" he said.

"Yeah," Charlie's voice answered.

"Well, cut it off, I gotta piss," Val told him. He started dancing up and down. "Ooh, ooh, ooh, ooh!" he whimpered.

"Use our bathroom," Liz told him.

"What a good idea," Val said in a peeping voice. Breathlessly humming "The Dance of the Hours" he hurried on tiptoe out of the living room.

"You all right, Charlie?" David called.

"Yeah, yeah," Charlie answered.

The tense silence between Max and Barbara was broken as she spoke to David. "About this war between the sexes, David," she said, "you said before 'in the beginning.' How far back does it go?"

"Our wedding day," Max said.

"Oh, fuck you," she snapped.

"That would be a novelty," he said.

"I gather no one cares if we get to the award show on time," David said, getting impatient now.

"It's not that late David," Liz told him, checking her wristwatch.

All right, to hell with it, David decided. *I'm* not up for an award.

"How far back does it go?" he began. "Heaven only knows. There are, for instance, two distinct versions of Creation in the Bible. One might be called the 'official' version. The other is man's. The first refers to male and female

48

in God's image. In the second, a mist goes up and man is made out of dust and woman out of man."

"A perfect description," Max said, nodding. "Women are second-hand dust."

"Oh, why don't you *stuff* it," Barbara told him.

Max's grin was cruel. "Right from the start, woman took from man. First, his rib. Then everything else. To quote the Mahabnarata—"

Barbara interrupted him, her expression distorted by hate. "You've spent so much time researching your distaste for women, it's no wonder you have no time for anything else," she said.

Max's voice went on over hers, speaking as though she hadn't. "'A wise man will avoid the contaminating society of women'," he quoted, "'as he would the touch of bodies infested by vermin.'"

"Lovely," Liz said, "Just lovely."

"I trust you're kidding, Max," David told him.

"I only kid for money," he replied.

"Well, you're full of it," Barbara said.

"You were saying David?" Liz said.

He looked at her pleadingly. Can't we *end* this? he thought.

"We're into it, David," Liz said. "This is no time to drop it."

"All *right*," he said, giving up. "At the dawn of civilization, society was set up along matriarchal lines."

"I'm back, you matriarchal fuckers," Val said, coming into the living room. "The pause that refreshes has refreshed."

David went on, trying to be oblivious to the air of tension in the room. "Giving birth, women were the dominant figures. Men provided food and shelter and defended the community. Everything else was female domain, including religion. God was female—born of nature, benevolent and wise. *Wicca* in the Celtic language—the word 'witch' came from it. Men couldn't understand that—or abide by it—so they declared it *bad*. Lilith for the Hebrews. Empusa for the Greeks, Lamia, the vampire. Woman draining and destructive."

"Right on," Max agreed.

Val grabbed his crotch and leered at Candy. "Drain this baby."

David felt a tremor of uneasiness at the way Ganine was looking at Val. If he was right about her, he thought.

"If women were considered to be so dangerous back then, why did men have anything to do with them?" Barbara asked.

"Pussy maybe?" Val said in a childlike voice. Barbara glared at him. Even Liz seemed less receptive to her brother's attempts at humor.

"Basically correct," David told him.

"See?" Val said to Barbara.

"If essentially offensive," David said. Val made a noise as though an arrow was piercing his heart.

"Sex runs second only to hunger need," David continued, not caring particularly now if they made the show or not. "To compensate, men kept women in their places with justifying rituals." He wondered how Liz felt about the awed expression on Ganine's face as she listened to him. "The male-oriented church defined witches as enemies. Religion lost its contact with nature and became a world power, a form of government. God came to represent not love but vengeance, all past ideas rejected. Including, naturally, female supremacy. Now the position of woman was below man."

"On top's not bad," Val said, pretending not to understand.

"In the Jewish, Christian and classical traditions, evil came into the world through women. David went on, "'From a woman, sin had it's beginning and because of her, we all die'. Ecclesiasticus."

Liz broke in. "How about the serpent drawing Eve into

50

temptation?" she said. "Everybody knows the snake is a phallic symbol."

"She didn't *have* to pick that apple." Max's tone was sly and goading.

"Right," Val said, maintaining the innocent, childlike voice. "She could have had a piece of celery. Oh, no, that's phallic too."

David continued as though neither Max nor Val had spoken. "The so-called Original Sin is a male concept of course. An excuse to set up a patriarchal system. Women confined to rearing families, leaving men to roam the world at will, venting their hostilities. Impaling animals for food—men for fun.

"As Hays put it, 'while women raised the children, men had time to put feathers in their hair, rattles on their wrists and ankles, to paint their faces and shape their egos in anyway that pleased them'."

"Now that's right on," Barbara said, nodding emphatically.

"Or as Grace Paley put it," David went on, "'Men used one foot to stand on women, the other foot to kick each other to death with.'"

"Undoubtedly," Liz said. "Thank God it doesn't work that way any more."

"I'm not so sure about that," David countered. "Men don't wear suits of armor any more or beat up women quite as freely. Generally speaking though—"

"*Candidly* speaking, you mean, "Val corrected.

"All right," David nodded. "Candidly speaking, things haven't really changed that much. Male attitudes remain pretty much the same.

"Civilization has been patriarchal for such a long time that the very definition of femininity is, as it always was, prejudiced, i.e., Masculine: strong and superior. Feminine: weak and inferior. In the standard dictionary, one of the definitions of the word 'female' is 'denoting simplicity, inferiority, weakness and the like'."

"Dictionaries prepared by men," Liz said.

"Of course," David agreed. "That's the point."

"If women were superior, they'd be our masters," Max said. "They're where they are because —" He broke off, grimacing.

"Because *what*?" Barbara challenged him.

"Forget it," Max said.

"No, let's hear your pearls of wisdom."

"I said *forget* it," Max's voice was tight.

"Look, why don't we just wind this up and limo to the theatre?" David said. "Let's not let this sour the entire evening. The bottom line is that we have, on our hands, an irrational system in which approximately half the human race regards the other half, at best, with condescension and suspicion, at worst with hatred and fear. Men, afraid of women, constantly creating an overall situation which perpetuates this pointless alienation. As I said this afternoon on my program, what women need right now is their own personal Lincoln. End of subject."

"End of acceptance too," Liz said. "We just don't buy it anymore."

"Nor should you," David responded.

"Yoko Ono said it all when she described women as the niggers of the world," Barbara added.

"Love that dark meat," Val said.

"You just don't get it, do you?" Barbara told him acidly. He made a face at her.

"Never mind a Lincoln for us," Liz said. "We'll take a Civil War if that's the way it has to be. I'll mount the goddamn barricades any day in the week."

"So will I!" Barbara said loudly. She looked at Max with scorn. "No retort?"

He scowled at her but said nothing, emptying his drink.

"Shall we change the subject now?" David suggested. "Go down and get our limo ride? I'm sure it's waiting for us."

"Men always want to change the subject when they're

losing," Barbara said, a smug smile on her lips.

"No one's winning, Babs," David told her.

"Hey, tell you what," Val broke in, grinning. "You wanna change the subject? Perfect. Before we go, I'll do Country Boy performing Hamlet's soliloquy."

"Oh, Jesus," Max muttered.

Liz was looking at her watch.

"It really *is* time to go," she told her brother.

"You said there was *time* before," Val argued.

"Maybe I'll join Charlie in the bathroom," Max said. "We can be nauseous together."

"Or full of shit together," Val said sharply. "Sit down you dumb fucker."

Val got up and moved to the open floor. "Okay, let's go," he shouted suddenly. "Charlie, get your crapping ass out here! I'm going to emote!"

There was no sound from Charlie. Liz got up and went to the bathroom door. "Are you all right, Charlie?" she asked.

"Yeah, I'll be right out," he told her in a grumbling voice.

"Well, let us know if you need anything," she said.

"Like a fucking cork for your asshole," Val said irritably.

Liz sat down again. Barbara was blowing out her breath, looking bored. David had to repress a smile. Max was sitting, looking sullen and uncomfortable. Ganine stared at Val. Candy was doing the same.

"All right, goddamn it, can I start now?" Val said. "You all know the set-up, Hamlet's mom is screwing his uncle who poured some toxic shit in his brother's ear—Hamlet's father."

"Perfect resume," Max said.

"Fuck off," Val told him. "Okay. Anyway, Hamlet wants to nail his uncle's ass but he's not sure about it which is why he does this soliloquy." He looked grave now. "Okay. It's just the lady director and Country Boy alone in this shit-house theatre in the middle of nowhere and the director's pissed off because Country Boy won't get in her pants so she tells him he's been doing the speech too artsy-fartsy all afternoon. She talks tough to him. 'Listen! *Kid!*' She's in her fucking forties, he's just thirty-three. So— 'Listen! *Kid!* Hamlet's just a *guy*. He's uptight. He's thinking about falling on his sword or cutting his throat or who knows what?' So he does this speech."

"Well, *do* it, Val," Liz told him.

"Okay, okay," he said irritably. "Just setting the god-damn scene for Chrissake."

He posed himself, attempting a noble expression, one hand held to his left temple. "*Christ*," Max mumbled.

"To be or not to be," Val started. "That's the question."

"That *is* the question," Max corrected.

"I *know* it's the fucking question, what are you inter-rupting me for?" Val lashed at him.

"Nothing." Max's voice was barely audible.

"Well, *fuck* off then!" Val snarled. Again he set himself. "To be or not to be," he started again, "that's the question. Whether it's nobler in your mind to suffer slings and arrows or take arms against a lot of troubles to end them."

"Jesus," Max murmured.

"Shut up already!" Val raged at him.

"Sorry."

"To die," Val continued, "To sleep. No more. And with some sleep to end the heartaches and the shocks that flesh has heir to—hair-do-doo-doo."

He broke off, frowning. "I didn't mean that," he said. "Where the fuck was I? Oh, yeah. The heartaches and the shocks. It's a consommé devoutly—"

"Consommé?" Liz asked.

"I meant *consummation*, damn it," Val said. "Lemme alone. It's a consummation to be wished devoutly. To die. To sleep. No more. And with sleep, to die, to sleep."

"You *said* that, Val," Liz told him.

"Well, Jesus Christ, it's the same fucking words twice in a row. What kind of shitass writer was this Shaykser anyway? Where the hell was I?"

Max muttered. "Dying."

"Screw off." Val took a deep breath and continued. "To die. Uh...to sleep. To weep. To bleep. Two sheep."

He blinked, starting, a look of confusion on his face. He stood there mutely.

"Val, are you—?" Liz started.

"I didn't mean to say that. Hold it, will ya?" He clenched his teeth and went on. "To sleep. Perch...perch... perch—*Jesus Christ*! What the fuck is that word?"

Liz looked concerned now. "Val."

"Just shut up!" Bracing himself, Val swallowed labouredly and forced himself to go on. "Okay. Maybe to dream. That's better anyway. Fucking Shaykser didn't know shit about writing for actors. Maybe to sleep. May *be* to sleep. Aye, there's the rub...a dub dub, three men in a tub. If the tub had been stronger—"

He stopped abruptly, looking alarmed now. "*What the fuck is going on?*" he asked.

David looked at him uneasily, then glanced at Ganine, but she looked as taken back as any of them were. Barbara's expression made it clear that she thought Val was attempting a poorly done gag. Liz's look indicated that she was inclined to agree with Barbara—except that Val looked genuinely upset by what was happening. Max sat slumped on his chair, wincing slightly.

"Val, come on," Liz began.

"Come on, shit!" he stormed at her. "I didn't say that!"

"Didn't say *what*?" she asked.

Val's voice overlapped hers. "Just...shut up, will you? Shut up." He forced himself to continue, his features tight with concentration. "Aye, there's the *rub*. For in that sleep of death, you have bad breath—"

He shook himself spasmodically and started in again before anyone could speak. "For in that sleep of death, what dreams may come when we have shuffled off to Buffalo.

God damn it!"

"Forget it, Val, we have to leave," Liz said.

"No, I won't forget it!" He was totally enraged now. "Just shut up!"

None of them knew how to react. Val was obviously rattled and infuriated by it as he set himself to finish the soliloquy no matter what.

His loss of control mounted steadily as he spoke. "When we have shuffled off to—this mortal coil must give us pause, the pause that refreshes—*must give us pause.* There's the respect that makes...makes...calamity, Howdy Calamity, it's me, Wild Bill."

Val's eyes were wild now, his expression that of a man struggling against impending madness. "Calamity of such a...such a...*Damn it!* Such a long life, long life, long, long, long, long, long life, *God damn!*"

"Val, *stop*," Liz said.

"Val, you'd better." David added.

Val went on as though no one had spoken, his voice tense and menacing. "For who would bear the whips and— scorns, whip me, baby, let me have it." His teeth clicked together. "I didn't say that," he forced himself on, "the whips and scorns, the warts and corns, no! Whips and scorns! Oppressions, wrong. Pangs of—laws delay—office —spurns—burns—urns—ferns—terns—turds, words, curds, birds, *God damn it to fucking goddamn hell!*"

He shuddered violently and released a wracking sob. Liz jumped up and tried to take his arm but he threw off her grip and lurched for the hallway. David stood and moved to grab him but Val was already at the door. Liz screamed his name as he flung open the hall door so violently that it crashed against the wall, knocking down two pictures.

Liz and David hurried after him. Candy struggled to her feet, looking confused and alarmed. She ran into the bedroom to get her jacket. Barbara sat immobile, staring in amazement toward the open doorway. Max stood slowly, weavingly, a strained expression on his face.

"Maybe we should help." Barbara said.

"*How* for Chrissake?" Max murmured.

Candy came running back, carrying her jacket. As she hurried toward the doorway, she pulled on the jacket. The instant she did, she cried out in terrified revulsion, thrashed about for several moments, then tore off the jacket and slung it to the floor, a gagging sound in her throat. Max and Barbara gaped at her as though she'd suddenly gone insane. Barbara stood on trembling legs. "*What's wrong?*" she asked.

"I don't know," Candy told her, starting to cry. "I just— I just—Oh, *God!*"

Barbara picked up the jacket. "You want to put it on?" she asked.

"*No!*" Candy looked repelled. She looked at the jacket Barbara held. She didn't want to touch it but was unable to leave without it. Moving abruptly to Barbara, she grabbed the jacket compulsively and ran from the apartment.

"Jesus Christ," Max said.

"What the hell is going on?" Barbara asked.

Liz came back in closing the hall door, a distraught look on her face. "What was *that?*" she asked, gesturing toward the door. "She went running by me as though she'd seen a ghost.

"No idea," Barbara said. "She went ballistic when she put her jacket on; she tore it off and wouldn't put it on again, then just grabbed it and ran. What's with Val?"

"I have no idea about *him* either," Liz said. "He seemed to go ballistic too."

"Is David with him?" Barbara asked.

"I guess he's going to drive Val home. He'll never make the awards. I doubt if any of us will. The limo's still waiting for us but—" She shrugged, sighing, disgustedly. "What a fucking night."

She and Barbara looked at Ganine. She still sat in her chair, expressionless.

Barbara was about to say something when the bathroom

door opened and Charlie came out. They all caught their breath. He looked ashen and infirm.

"What's wrong, Charlie?" Liz asked.

He didn't speak at first. Then he said, "I think—"

He was unable to finish... Suddenly, he gagged and clapped his right hand over his mouth. They gasped as blood began to spurt between his fingers. He staggered forward with a choking sound. Liz moved quickly to assist him but, before she could reach him, Charlie stumbled and collapsed, a hoarse cry in his throat. Liz cried his name and kneeled beside him. He was already unconscious, bleeding from the mouth.

"Jesus Christ, what's going on?" Max said. He sounded frightened now too.

Suddenly, simultaneously, Barbara and Liz looked at Ganine, their expressions equally suspicious and uneasy. Ganine was motionless, pushed back against the chair cushion, staring at Charlie.

On her face, a look of abject terror.

FRIDAY

STATION KBNY. Doctor David Harper: *Candidly Speaking.* How can I help you?

Doctor, you said that woman's lib is failing. I'd like to know what you see as a result of this.

I haven't any simple answer for that, I'm afraid. In nineteen sixty-eight, however—*sixty-eight*, mind you—in the American Journal of Psychotherapy, Doctor Natalie Shainess wrote that women are losing contact with their inner selves and, as a consequence of this, becoming increasingly alienated from meaningful life. Unhappily, this alienation persists today. More than persists, grows more extreme each year.

Expressing itself in what way, Doctor?

For one thing, women seem to be putting sex out of their

61

minds or turning to other women for it.

That startles me, Doctor. Is that, statistically, correct?

It is. And this widespread increase of bisexuality and lesbianism could be the forefront of a coming insurgence, women turning away from men in every way, tired of living on men's terms. Simply stated, women are sick and tired of being what men want them to be. They want to be what *they* want to be.

You worry me, Doctor. Are there any other signs of this insurgence?

Yes, there are. Women seem to be turning their backs on life itself as dictated by men. Each year, more than fifty million abortions are performed in the world. This is more than mere disenchantment.

I feel defensive now. Are women to blame for this?

Not at all. They have every right to resent the fact that, in order to achieve parity in the world, they've been forced to distort their basic nature, becoming some sort of in-between sex that suffers male afflictions—high blood pressure, ulcers, nervous breakdowns, heart attacks—but rarely enjoys male advantages. To quote Esther Harding; by organizing and conventionalizing herself, a woman has cut herself off from the springs of life which lie in the depths of her being.

Is that what *you* think is happening to women?

Candidly speaking, yes. I think too many women are losing direction by ignoring their inner rhythms and trying to match the inner rhythms of men. What can possibly be worse than being dominated by men? Answer: Being dominated by the essence of maleness.

Are men and women really that much different, Doctor?

I believe they are. To women, life is cyclic, a force that ebbs and flows in her, not only in daily rhythms but in monthly ones as well. In the course of one lunar cycle, a woman's energy waxes, shines, then wanes. These changes affect not only her physical and sexual life, but her psychic life as well; Esther Harding again.

So what can women do to regain their…inner rhythms, as you call them?

Frankly, I don't know. The trouble is that, now-a-days, women seem disinclined to look into their own fundamental natures. They erect a barrier of will between their outward and inner selves. And it's this inner self—whatever you choose to call it—that's been 'turned sour', if you will, by eons of mistreatment and misunderstanding.

Do men have any idea that all this is going on?

Some think they do. It's primarily intellectualized, though. Little emotional intuition involved. That's why, to the greater majority of men, women are bewildering and vexing creatures, beyond their comprehension. And, yet, they're so much more. Cavendish in *Man, Myth and Magic* describes them as—quote—in touch with reality through a secret sympathy with the heart of things—unquote.

Can these differences ever be reconciled, Doctor?

They *have* to be. Men and women need each other. And, yet, their aims are so divergent that the conflict could prove irreconcilable.

What then? Revolution?

As a social movement? No. This runs deeper.

11:39 A.M.

"I DON'T KNOW *what* to think," Liz said.

She and David were sitting on the living room sofa in their pajamas, having coffee and pastries. On the radio, a Mozart symphony was playing softly.

"I don't either," David admitted. "It's damn strange though. What happened to Val, what happened to Charlie. I just can't make myself believe this girl had anything to do with either occurrence. And then to find out that she doesn't live in this building at all. It's too bizarre."

"It *is*," Liz agreed. "I keep thinking of the look on her face. Blind terror."

"Well, that's not surprising. She *is* disturbed in some way we can't possibly evaluate. What happened to your brother and Charlie probably terrified her."

"I suppose," Liz said, "what happened to Charlie isn't

that surprising though, the way he eats and drinks, his being over-weight. It's what happened to Val that really disturbs me."

"Have you spoken to him this morning?"

"He didn't answer his phone. I left a message." She sighed deeply. "Anyway, let's forget about what happened. I'd like to talk about the show again. "It would have been nice if we'd been able to pick up those three Emmys in person."

"I know," he sympathized. "I'm really sorry about that. You deserved to be there."

"Even though the show is drivel?" she asked, her voice tightened.

"Let's not go back to that again," he said.

"I think we *should* go back to that," Liz disagreed. "What you don't seem to realize—and *never have*—" she cut off his attempted objection—"is that I am fully aware—as all of us are, that *Country Boy* is basically designed for morons. Morons who create a nice healthy rating though. Morons whose votes got us three damn Emmys."

"I *am* aware of that, Liz," David said. "But what *you* don't seem to be aware of—or more likely, refuse to admit—is that the premise of the series is the denigration of women."

"Oh, come on David," Liz said with a faint smile. "You're making too much of it."

"Liz, *Country Boy* constantly makes fools of women. Really, I'm amazed at the show's ratings considering that a large proportion of the viewers has to be women."

"David, *come on*," Liz said. "The show is childlike. Country Boy is an idiot. If he demeans women, it only reflects on him, makes *him* look stupid, not the women he makes fun of."

David shrugged. "I still don't understand your acceptance of the show. You of all people."

"It doesn't *bother* me, David, because I'm *above* it," she said. "I'm successful. I make good money. I'm acquiring more and more influence in the business. That's enough for me. Who gives a damn what the show's about? I'll leave it when something better comes along. That's how much I think of *Country Boy.*"

David sighed. "Okay," he said.

Liz bristled at his tone. "It's perfectly all right for a man to make money any way he pleases," she said accusingly. "No one questions that."

"I question it," David told her.

"All right, you're an exception. Congratulations," she said coolly. "The point is—I'm making it in a chauvinistic world. I think that's pretty damn good."

"Of course it is," he said. "You know I'm proud of your accomplishment."

"Then stop hassling me," she snapped.

He wanted to let it go. But her attitude disturbed him. "You're talking a lot about chauvinism these days," he told her.

"Yeah, well there's a lot of it going around," she said sarcastically.

"And yet you defer to your brother who's as chauvinistic as they come," he said.

"He's a baby," Liz said. "I don't take him seriously."

"A baby what?" he asked. "Viper?"

She started to speak but he cut her off. "You have such strong convictions about being a woman and yet you let him insult women right in front of you."

"That's because I identify with his male aggressiveness. *Right?*"

David frowned at her. "Did I say that?"

"I know you think I've changed and you don't like the change. I'm not the sweet liberal Elizabeth you married. I'm ballsy Liz now."

"If that's how you prefer to see yourself," he said, his voice mildly scolding.

"Well, isn't it true?" she demanded. "I used to give a lot of credence to 'justice for all.' Now I'm out for myself because no one in this world is going to help me otherwise."

He didn't speak, looking at her with a distressed expression. Then he murmured, "*No one?*"

She was about to speak, then sighed and looked repentant. "I'm sorry," she said. "I know you're on my side."

He smiled and, leaning over, kissed her lightly on the cheek. She returned the smile and was about to say something when the telephone rang.

"More bad news, no doubt," she said. David smiled a little sadly.

Liz picked up the receiver. "Hello?"

She listened. "Yes, Catherine," she said. Listened again. Her features tightened. "Oh, my God," she said. She listened, nodding. "I'll come over as soon as I can."

She hung up, looking at David with a grim expression. "What is it?" he asked.

"That was Charlie's ex-wife. The bleeding won't stop. He's in the hospital."

"Oh, no." He grimaced. "Poor guy." He shook his head. "He always looked so rugged."

"He always seemed to be." Liz stood. "Obviously, he wasn't." She started for the bedroom. "I'm going over to see him."

David stood up. "I'll go with you."

"You don't have to," she said. "You barely know him."

"*Liz.* I'll go with you."

"All right, fine," she said distractedly. She moved into the bedroom to get dressed.

David started to follow her. He'd only taken a few steps when his right ankle twisted abruptly and he stumbled, almost falling. "Oh! Jesus!" he cried.

"What is it?" she called.

"My *ankle*," he told her, "I think I sprained it." He tried to stand on it and cried out hollowly. "*No,*" he said.

Hissing with pain, he limped to the nearest chair and slumped down on it. He twisted his right foot experimentally, crying out again.

Liz came back into the living room. "You sprained your *ankle?*" she asked. She sounded as though she couldn't believe it.

"Yeah," he said, his teeth set on edge.

"Well, for Christ's sake," Liz said, her tone still dubious. "You can't *stand* on it?"

"I don't think so." David tried again to move his right foot. "*Ooh*," he said, eyes closing from the pain.

She came over to the chair. "Are you going to be all right?" she asked.

"I suppose," he said. "I don't think I'm going to be able to go with you though."

"It's just as well," she said.

He looked at her irritably. "What do you mean?" he asked.

"Well, you don't really know Charlie," she said. "Anyway," she cut him off, "you're supposed to go to that conference this afternoon, aren't you? Are you going to be able to make that?"

"Jesus, I don't know," he muttered.

She looked at him indecisively. "Well, maybe—" she began.

"No, no, go ahead," he anticipated her remark. "I'll be all right, don't worry about it. Go see Charlie. And tell him how sorry I am."

"Yeah," she said, she looked at him questioningly for another few moments, then moved over and kissed him on top of the head. "You'll be all right?" she asked.

"I'll be fine. I won't be tap-dancing but I'll manage."

She smiled a little, "All right," she said, "Just...stay off it."

"I will." He managed to return her smile.

"I'll call you from the hospital to see how you're doing," she told him.

"Just call to tell me how Charlie is," he said.

She nodded and went back into the bedroom. Wincing and hissing again, David got up and lurched to the sofa, slumping down on it. He worked his right foot out of its slipper, groaning softly as he did, then lay back on the sofa, propping his right leg on a pillow. "*Whoa*," he mumbled. He felt like an idiot for doing this. He hadn't sprained his ankle for years. "Perfect time to do it," he mumbled.

Fifteen minutes later, Liz came out of the bedroom, wearing a skirt and a jacket over her sweater. "I'll come back as soon as possible," she told him. "And I'll call from the hospital to see how you're doing."

"Okay." He nodded.

As she left the apartment, David leaned back on a sofa pillow he placed under his head. "*Idiot*," he murmured. He looked concerned. How could he possibly make that conference now? And he'd canceled his appearance on the radio, having them play a recording made yesterday. "Dear God," he complained. "One thing after another." He closed his eyes. Did he have an ankle brace he could wear? He didn't think so.

He opened his eyes, hearing a knock on the door.

"What's the matter, did you forget something?" he called.

There was no reply. Another knock.

"Is it *locked*?" he asked loudly.

"I don't know," he thought Liz answered.

"I *hope* not!" he said. "I can't get over there right now!"

The door opened and Ganine came in, wearing a tweed skirt and a snug beige sweater under her jacket.

For several seconds, David couldn't speak. The sight of her was so disconcerting to him.

"Ganine, you can't come in," he told her. "I'm sorry but you'll have to leave."

She closed the door, looking at him pleadingly.

"Ganine, I *mean* it," he said, scowling.

She moved toward the sofa. "Are you hurt?" she asked.

"Ganine—!" He felt angrily frustrated. "You *cannot* come in!" Impulsively, he tried to stand but fell back with a cry of pain.

"You *are* hurt," she said, a disturbed look on her face.

"Ganine, *please?*" he asked. He felt helpless as she crossed the living room. "*I cannot* talk to you now." He felt an undercurrent of uneasiness about her being there.

"I can help you," she told him.

"Oh, for God's sake," he said. "*I need to be alone.*"

"Please, I can help you," she said.

He felt a shudder up his back. *Now* what was she going to do? he wondered. He felt increasingly nervous about her, about what she seemed capable of doing.

"Did you hurt your ankle?" she asked. He had the sudden feeling that she'd *made* it happen. That was ridiculous though. He wouldn't allow himself to succumb to such a childish notion. "Yes. I did," he said. "Now will you please go? I can't talk with you right now."

It was as though he hadn't spoken. "My father hurt his ankle once and I rubbed it and it got better," she told him. She kneeled beside the sofa, smiling at him timidly.

"Really, Ganine—" he said, starting to feel strangely helpless.

He gasped in pain as she put her hands around his ankle, realizing, at that moment that he was actually afraid of her. He tried to repress the feeling but couldn't. "What are you doing?" he asked in a weak voice.

"Just lie still," she told him, sounding like a little girl playing mother.

"Ganine, that *hurts,*" he said. He didn't like the feeling of ineffectiveness he could not control.

Abruptly, he looked startled. "It feels funny," he said without thinking.

"I know," she said. "That's because it's getting better."

He wanted to contest what she was saying but was unable to do so. He stared at her small, white hands as they rubbed, almost caressingly, around his ankle.

He felt, suddenly, incredulous. "My God," he murmured. The pain was clearly diminishing. He wanted to tell her but still felt the same nervous uneasiness about her.

"It's better, isn't it?" she said. It was not a question.

He had to speak. "Yes," he told her. "It is." Regardless of his continuing apprehension about her, he felt a surge of physical comfort. "It's incredible."

"No, it's not," she said. "I can do it all the time."

David felt that this was the obvious time to question her about her unusual—some might consider it miraculous—power. Amazement—and relief at the ending of pain—was now becoming a need to understand what strange abilities she seemed to possess. *Seemed*? he thought. They were real.

He didn't know how to start though. "You've...done this before?" he asked.

"I told you, with my father," she answered, her expression one of almost smugness. It irritated him but, somehow, he didn't dare react adversely to it.

"The pain is gone now," she told him. "You can walk." She removed her hands from his ankle.

"That's...it?" he asked uncertainly.

"Yes." She nodded, smiling. "You can *walk* now."

He hesitated, then had to be sure that, what seemed to have happened, really had. Tentatively, he started rising to his feet, putting weight on his ankle gingerly.

Damn, he thought. It had really happened. The pain was completely gone.

"See?" she said. "I *told* you."

He walked around a little bit. "I will be damned," he said, looking amazed. Ganine smiled. "I'm glad I helped you," she told him.

"Did you pass my wife in the hall?" he asked.

She looked taken back by the question but shook her head. "I didn't see her."

He couldn't imagine how that was possible. But if Liz had seen her, she obviously would have come back and more likely locked the door. He'd have to accept what Ganine had said.

It occurred to him then. "Why did you tell me you lived in this building?" he asked.

She looked embarrassed. "I was afraid that, if I didn't, you might not have talked to me," she said.

That didn't make sense to him but, once more, he hesitated to confront her in any way. "Have you…demonstrated this ability of yours to anyone else?" he asked.

"No," she said. "Only you." Her smile was—he could not avoid the observation—undeniably tender. "I have to like the person."

Something about the way she said it made him uneasy again. He remembered what happened to Val, even—as much as he wanted to avoid the thought—Charlie. Could she do harmful things as well as what she did for him? He stared at her with no idea what to say.

"Where did your wife go?" Ganine asked.

An involuntary shudder laced across his back. Why did she want to know? Could he avoid answering her? He felt uneasy about that too.

"To the hospital," he told her. "A friend of ours is there."

"The man who fell down last night?" she said, wincing at her memory of it. "Who had blood coming out of his mouth?"

Suddenly, David wanted very much to get rid of her. Despite what she'd done to his ankle and despite her obvious—that was almost unnerving as well—*affection* for him, he was totally uncomfortable with her again. There was something about her…something *dark*. He could not control the thought. What was it though?

He realized that, while thinking all that, he had told her that, yes, it was Charlie in the hospital. He felt a compulsion to ask her if she'd had anything to do with what happened to Charlie. He was afraid to ask though.

"Can you help me now?" Ganine asked him.

"Well," he started awkwardly, "As I told you yesterday—"

"*Please*," she said plaintively. "I *need* your help."

He was going to tell her again that it was impossible when it occurred to him that Ganine was someone far out of the ordinary. Maybe he owed it to himself to understand her better. Owed it to—was that ostentatious?—the medical community.

"Well, I'll try—" he started, breaking off at her sudden smile of gratitude. He had to keep her properly informed, not let her believe that he could really help her.

"I'll talk with you for a little while," he said, realizing that intimidation was as much motivated in him as a genuine desire to help her. "Then I'll *have* to send you to the therapist I mentioned. I just don't practice anymore."

She looked displeased, which made him feel uncomfortable again. "You do on the radio," she said.

His smile was pained. "That's different, Ganine," he said. "Very brief analyses for many people. Nothing in depth."

"I know you can help me," she insisted.

He hesitated, then drew in a deep, sighing breath. "All right," he said. "Let's see what we can do."

Her smile was one of a childlike joy. Already, he felt that this attempt to help her was, very likely, going to prove fruitless.

He gestured toward the sofa and she moved to sit down quickly, an eager look on her face. Oh, God, I hope this isn't a terrible mistake, David thought. What made him think he could help her? And was he doing it entirely because of how she'd healed his ankle?

He sat on a chair across from her suddenly aware that he was still in his pajamas. He knew he should dress first but he didn't want to delay the—what? *Treatment?* The notion displeased him.

"Aren't you going to sit next to me?" Ganine asked. The observation was unavoidable; her tone and smile were definitely suggestive.

"It isn't done that way, Ganine," he told her.

She gazed at him entreatingly, then—he saw her facial change—accepted what he'd said.

"All right, what is it that's bothering you?" he asked.

"There's something…"

She didn't finish, looking uncertain.

"Yes?" he asked.

"Something…" She drew in a shuddering breath— "*drawing* at me, *filling* me," she finished.

"Physically?" he asked. "Or psychologically?"

"I don't know what that means," she told him.

"How would *you* describe it then?" he asked.

"It's…something…inside me. *Way* inside me."

"How does it express itself?" he asked.

He saw that she didn't understand that question either. "I mean…how does it make you feel?"

"Not real," she said immediately. "As if…as if…I'm not *me* anymore."

"You feel like someone else?"

Ganine stared at him in silence.

"Never mind that question," he said. "I don't really understand what you've said. What exactly do you mean, you're not *you* anymore." Possession? he thought. Multiple personality?

"I just don't feel like *me* anymore," she said. "There's something *inside* me. Something *strong*. Something I don't like."

"Do you…feel that this something is what gives you a kind of—*power*?" David asked.

"I don't know." she murmured. She looked on the verge of tears.

"Okay, okay, let that go," David told her. "We can—"

"There's something else," she said. She looked suddenly embarrassed. David thought that she was about to complete her statement. Then, visibly bracing herself, she said, "My period stopped two months ago."

Oh, God, David thought. Was that what this was all about? An unwanted pregnancy? "I'm really not equipped to—" he began.

She broke in, her tone distressed and—he could not interpret it in any other way—*angry*. "I haven't let anyone touch me in almost three years," she said.

David didn't know how to respond to that. After several moments of non-plused silence, he said, "Have you been to a family doctor?"

"I don't *have* one," she told him, looking pained.

"Have you been to *any* doctor?" he asked.

"*No*," she said. "But I'm going to have a baby. I know it."

Oh, boy, he thought, now a false pregnancy. What more can she have to tell him?

"But I *can't* be having a baby," Ganine said in a frightened voice. "I know that too."

David was uncertain as to whether he should broach the subject or not. Then he had to accept the fact that there was nothing else he *could* say. "You *are* aware," he told her, "that there are various psychological conditions which create apparent pregnancy."

"*That's not what it is*," she said, almost angrily.

David blew out breath. Now what? he thought.

He tensed in surprise as Ganine began to cry, beginning with a broken sob.

"I'm not a bad girl," she insisted. "I didn't do anything. I swear I didn't."

"Okay. I believe you," David reassured her.

It didn't seem to help. Her crying increased. She sounded heartbroken. David frowned, wondering what to do.

Finally, he rose from the chair and moved to the sofa, sitting next to her. He patted her back, trying to comfort her. "It's all right," he said, gently. "You don't have to cry."

He stiffened, teeth, suddenly on edge, as she pressed against him, clinging to his arm. "I'm not bad," she said in a wavering voice. "I'm *not*."

"No, of course you're not," he told her. "You're just—"

His voice choked off as Ganine pressed against him more tightly, sliding her arms around him like a frightened child. He was aware, in an instant, of her body against his, the fact that he was wearing only pajamas and—it seemed an absurd observation—that the music on the radio was Tchaikowsky's *Romeo and Juliet.*

"It's okay, Ganine," he heard himself say; it sounded like the voice of someone else. His arms, to his alarmed surprise, had slipped around her body. This is crazy, he thought. He tried to draw his arms away but found himself unable to do it. Oh, now *stop* this, he heard a warning voice in his head.

He couldn't get his arms away. To his distress—it almost felt like fear now—his arms were tightening around Ganine. No, this is wrong, it's *crazy*, the voice in his head insisted. But he couldn't stop himself. "It's okay," the voice—was it *his*? He wondered apprehensively—kept saying it over and over. "It's okay, Ganine. Okay."

Her sobbing was gradually stilling. He became uncomfortably aware that she was starting to breathe more heavily, moving—was it *writhing*?—against him. David tried—it was struggle, he realized with chilled alarm—to draw away from her but simply couldn't. He became intensely aware of how thin his cotton pajama bottoms were and what was happening involuntarily to his lower body.

"Ganine, *no*," he said, stunned by the weakness of his voice. He tried, in vain, to disengage himself from her, aware in dismay, as he did, that his effort was ineffective, almost futile. What *is* this? he thought, his brain in near panic now.

The music—was it an accident? Disturbing coincidence?—kept rising in volume, sounding more passionate by the moment. It was not imagination, he was distressingly aware that Ganine was clinging to him, writhing more and more, her small breasts rubbing against his chest. This is *insanity*! his brain cried out.

The warning was in vain. The music was nearing its peak. Her arms were holding him; they felt incredibly strong. His arms kept tightening; against his will, he knew. He couldn't pull away from her. But whether the rise of physical demand was causing it—or something more deeply menacing—he had no way of knowing.

All he was intensely aware of was her tear-streaked face tilting back to gaze at him, her expression one of—no matter how he sought to deny the realization—desire. No, this is *impossible*! the voice protested furiously.

Without success. His breathing, now like hers, was obviously straining. Her eyes were blue, he saw. He hadn't noticed it before. They were attractive eyes, compelling eyes. If only—

The transition came so suddenly, it made his heartbeat lurch. Abruptly, with a feeble moan of surrender, he lowered his face to hers.

Her lips were soft, available. Her clutching arms were not soft. This is crazy! the voice kept insisting in his mind. Even as his lips pressed hard against hers, even as he accepted the parting of those lips, the moist warmth of her tongue darting into his mouth. Oh, God, this is *insane*! he thought—with no ability to end the kiss, his arms embracing her rigidly, aware of the uncontrollable stirring in his loins.

It was Ganine, not him, who jerked away with sudden force and, strangely it occurred to him, it was as though resolve returned to him. She pressed her cheek to his, her murmuring impassioned. "I love you, I love you, I love you."

The mechanical repetition of the words completed the piercing of whatever clouding of his will he believed had taken place. He pulled away from her.

"No, that's impossible," he said, startled by the husky sound of his voice.

"It's *not*," she said, reaching for him. "I love you, David."

"*No*, Ganine." He put his hands on her shoulders and held her away. "You have to understand. This is *impossible*."

"If I let you have my body, will you help me?" she asked eagerly.

The total madness of her words drove him further from her. "Ganine, this has got to stop," he said. *"Right now."*

"You *kissed* me," she said. "I know you want my body. I *know* it."

"No, I *don't."* He looked at her severely. "This is all a mistake."

"No, it's *not*," she said. "I know the way you kissed me."

He stood as quickly as he could and moved to the telephone, shaken by the weakness in his legs. "I'm going to—" he began.

"No, David," she broke in. "I know you want me. I *know* it."

He interrupted her. "I am going to give you the number of the woman therapist I told you about. She can—"

"No, David!" she said despairingly. "I need *your* help!"

"I'm sorry, that's impossible," he told her. He grimaced in aggravation. The address book wasn't in the drawer of the telephone table. "It must be in the bedroom," he muttered.

"I don't *want* her!" Ganine cried out like a frustrated child.

"I'm sorry, I just—" His voice died off as he moved toward the bedroom. "Stay here," he said to her.

"No! I *won't!"* she cried.

He didn't look at her as he walked into the bedroom.

"David, *no!"* she almost yelled the words.

He walked to Liz's side of the bed and opened its table drawer. The address book wasn't in it. *"Damn,"* he muttered, starting to circle the bed.

He froze at the loud noises in the living room, the sudden stopping of the radio music. "Now what?" he said. He heard the sound of Ganine's running footsteps and started to return to the living room. Before he could reach it, he flinched at the crashing sound of the hall door being violently slammed. For a moment, he felt a twinge of guilt but almost immediately, a sense of relief made him sigh. Thank

God, she's gone, he thought.

The radio had been thrown to the floor and the plate of pastries and both coffee cups had been flung across the floor staining the carpet. Jesus God, that timid little girl had quite a temper. Timid? his mind contested. It was not a descriptive word for Ganine. He blew out heavy breath. At least she was gone. That was a blessing.

He began to pick up the fallen pastries and platter, the coffee cups, one of them was cracked; one of Liz's favorites. Well, that would have to do. Cleaning up the coffee stains was more of a problem.

5:39 P.M.

It was almost dark as Liz unlocked the door and entered the apartment. Switching on two lamps, she put down her purse on the sofa and turned for the bar. She needed a drink. After today, a drink was definitely in order, she thought. She poured herself a third of a glass of vodka and turned toward the kitchen for some ice cubes. "Oh, to hell with it," she muttered. Stopping, she took a long swallow of the room temperature vodka. I need alcohol, not ice, she thought.

She was taking a second swallow when she noticed it. She stood motionless for several seconds, then crossed to the kitchen and flicked up the light switch.

For nearly thirty seconds, she stared at the hanging plants, a blank expression on her face, unable to comprehend what she was looking at.

Every plant was richly green with not a speck of brown on any leaf.

Something about the sight unnerved her. Putting her glass of vodka on the counter between the rooms, she moved to one of the hanging plants and examined it closely.

She started to reach for it, to touch it, she realized. All she could do was stare at it in silence. I'm gaping, she thought. The change in the plants was not pleasing, it only made her feel uneasy. She tensed as an involuntary shudder laced up her back. "What the *hell?*" she murmured. This was impossible. Yet it had happened, the change was right in front of her. Where there had been brown-edged dying plants, there were new plants that seemed to be bursting with new-growth vitality.

Liz jerked around, catching her breath as the door to the master bathroom opened and footsteps moved across the bedroom. "David?" she said.

There was no answer. Liz felt herself tighten. "David, is that you?" she asked.

Ganine appeared in the doorway.

Wearing David's terrycloth robe. Liz stared at her, stunned. Unable to summon anger. The sight of Ganine—she could not avert it—frightened her. Her brain tumbled with unanswerable questions. What was Ganine doing in the apartment? Why was she wearing David's bathrobe? Where *was* David for that matter?

The huskiness of her voice alarmed her. "What are you doing here?" she asked, immediately thinking: Why am I even *talking* to her? Why aren't I grabbing her and throwing her out of the apartment?

Ganine's reply was wary, what she said alarming Liz even further. "I'm sorry," she said. "I didn't think you'd be back so soon." She sounded genuinely apologetic.

"You didn't think—?" Liz couldn't finish the response, her voice choking off. She cleared her throat. *"Where's my husband?"* she demanded.

"He left a long time ago," Ganine told her. "He was going to some conference."

Liz shuddered. *Then why are you here?* she thought, and she tightened. *"Why are you wearing my husband's bathrobe?"* she demanded. Don't talk to her! her mind stormed.

Ganine's reply staggered her. "I have no clothes on," she said.

Liz found herself moving suddenly for the bedroom.

Ganine stepped aside, looking frightened. Liz froze in the bedroom doorway, looking at the bed.

The sheets were rumpled, one of them hanging off the mattress edge. Liz felt her stomach muscles jerking in, a feeling of nausea suddenly overwhelming her. She twisted around to look at Ganine; she knew that she was glaring. *"How long have you been here?"* she asked, barely able to speak.

"Since early afternoon," Ganine said. The calmness of her voice made Liz shudder with rage. Ganine's answer had been quiet and completely non-apologetic, a simple statement of fact. "I fell asleep."

Liz struggled for control. *"Get out of here,"* she said, barely able to speak.

"I can't," Ganine replied. "I have to see your husband. He said he'd help me."

"Help you?" Liz felt herself unable to react coherently. She only knew that she wanted Ganine out of the apartment.

"I'll leave after I see him," Ganine said casually.

"No, you'll leave right now," Liz told her.

"I can't," Ganine replied.

"Would you like me to call the police?" Liz threatened, trembling, feeling ill.

Ganine looked alarmed. "The *police?*" she said.

Liz fought for control. "You're intruding in my home," she said in a low, shaken voice. "Get out or, so help me God, I'll have you *taken* out."

Ganine only stared at her, her expression one of disbelief.

"You *hear* me?" Liz raged.

"Don't do this," Ganine told her pleadingly. "I can't—"

"Get out of here!" Liz shouted at her. "God damn you! *Out!*"

Ganine flinched, started to speak, then couldn't. Liz stepped aside as Ganine moved hurriedly into the bedroom. Liz shuddered violently as she saw Ganine throw off the bathrobe. She was naked underneath.

Unable to control the shaking of her body, Liz watched

as Ganine snatched up her dress from the floor and pulled it over her head. She stepped into her shoes. Liz shuddered again as she saw Ganine pick up her bra and panties—they were red—and her jacket and start back towards the living room.

Liz turned and stalked across the living room to throw open the hall door. If I had a gun, she thought as Ganine hurried towards her.

At the doorway, Ganine stopped and tried to speak. Liz wouldn't let her. *"And don't ever let me see you here again,"* she said, teeth clenched, a murderous expression on her face.

Ganine tried again to say something but, again, Liz cut her off. "You *hear* me?!" she cried.

Ganine's face was tight and pale. Repressing a sob, she moved into the hall and Liz slammed the door behind her, stood there, shaking. "Bitch," she muttered, then exploded. *"Bitch!"*

She was turning back towards the living room when the pain flared in her head. Gasping, she clutched at her skull with both hands. It felt as though a white-hot knife had stabbed at her brain.

"Jesus Christ," she muttered, her eyes gone wild with dread. "It *is* her! It *is!"* Stumbling to a chair, she fell down on it, whining in pain. Who *was* Ganine? *What* was she? Liz felt weak and helpless, turning her head from side to side, a groan of agony pulsing in her throat.

She managed to reach the bathroom cabinet and pull it open. Her hands were shaking so badly that her pain pills scattered from their vial into the toilet. She managed to swallow three of them, gulping them down without water, then, labouredly, her face distorted by the pain, started back toward the living room.

Afraid that she was going to lose her balance and fall, she managed to work her way back to the living room—she couldn't go near the bed with its obvious tangle of sheets, David's bathrobe on top of them.

She sank down on the sofa, planning to lie down. She couldn't do it though. She sat there, slumped, both hands against her head, her eyes closed.

Once, she opened them and found herself staring at the lush greenery of the hanging plants in the kitchen. With a revulsed sound, she closed her eyes again. It's me, she tried to believe. It's stress, it's fury at what that bitch has done. She couldn't convince herself, however. Groaning softly at the aching in her head, she tried to tell herself to relax. Relax, she thought. *Relax.*

It didn't work. She began to cry softly, warm tears trickling down her cheeks. Please come home, she thought, even though she knew that her rage was also directed at David.

After forty minutes, the headache had abated slightly, the pain not searing but a dull, throbbing ache. Liz managed to reach out for the telephone and, carefully, punch out a number, one hand remaining pressed to her head.

After five unanswered rings on the other end of the line, the answering service cut in.

"Please tell Miss Regina that Val Bettinger's sister returned her call," she told the woman.

Hanging up, she punched out another number. There was no answer. After five rings, another answering service spoke.

"Please tell Mr. Bettinger that his sister called again," she instructed.

Putting down the receiver, she put her other hand to her head. *What was it?* she wondered. How could Ganine possibly give her such a violent headache! It seemed beyond belief. And yet—

The thought broke off as the hall door opened and David came in. He looked surprised to see her on the sofa, both hands held against her skull.

"Another headache?" he asked in concern.

She didn't answer, staring at him balefully. "Was that girl here again?" he asked, crossing the room.

"Don't play cunning with me," she said.

"What?" He stared at her in confusion.

"*You* tell *me* if she was here," Liz told him.

"What do you mean? I don't understand." David sat beside her on the sofa, startled by her abrupt shrinking away from him. "What's *wrong*?" he asked.

"*You* tell *me*," she repeated.

"Liz, you're just *confusing* me," he said. "Please tell me what's going on. Has Ganine been here again? Is that why you're having another headache?"

"God damn it, David," Liz said tensely. "Don't play games with me."

"*Games*?" He stared at her, his expression one of utter bafflement. "You aren't making sense," he said. "I'm really sorry that you're having another headache but I just don't know what the hell you're talking about."

Her teeth were clenched as she answered, "I'll spell it out for you then," she said. "*Check the bedroom.*"

"Check—?" His voice broke off; he stared at her uncomprehendingly. "The—"

"The *bed*, God damn it! The *bed*!" She started crying again, half in fury, half in pain.

He started to say something else, then, instead, stood and walked to the bedroom. He looked inside, frowning in puzzlement. "Why did you tear up the bed? I made it before I left."

"I warn you, David," she threatened.

"Liz, *what are you talking about*?" he said.

She struggled for control. "*I'm talking about the fucking bed*," she told him. "And I mean it literally!"

David was speechless, he looked at the bed, at Liz, at the bed again, at Liz. Then it hit him. The *headache* again.

"She *has* been here," he said.

"Oh, bravo, bravo," Liz snarled. "You finally got it."

He stared at her in silence. Suddenly, he knew what she was saying. "You think—?" He broke off, incredulous, "You think that Ganine and I—?" Again, he broke off. "Liz are you *insane*? How could you possibly?"

She interrupted fiercely. "She was here when I got back! Wearing your bathrobe! *Naked* underneath!"

"Jesus Christ," he muttered. He shook his head in disbelief. "And you assumed—?"

"*Assumed!*" she screamed. The effort made her cry out in pain.

"Liz, I don't know why you're thinking this," he said, "but you are absolutely wrong! She *was* here this morning. I tried to give her Dr. Thorston's number and she left in a fury! Fifteen minutes later, I made our bed, got dressed and attended the conference! *All afternoon*, Liz! *All afternoon*! I just got back! How in the hell am I supposed to have had sex with that demented girl! For that matter, how did she get back inside the apartment?! I locked the door when I left."

Liz stared at him with a dumbfounded expression. "I don't—" she started, then couldn't finish. "David, I don't... understand."

"I don't understand either," he responded. "Except—" He stopped and pulled a sheet of paper from his jacket pocket, bringing it over to Liz. "The schedule of events this afternoon," he said. "In case you still need proof that I wasn't here."

She took the paper and glanced at it, then put it down on her lap. David walked over to the sofa and sat beside her. He put his right arm over her shoulders. At first she stiffened resistingly, then the tension slipped out of her and she put her head on his shoulder. "What are we going to do?" she asked.

"About Ganine?"

She didn't answer.

"I have no idea at the moment," he said. "Except that we've got to avoid her. If she can give you a headache..."

"That isn't all she can do," Liz said. "Look at the plants."

Like her, he couldn't believe his eyes at first. Then he muttered, "Jesus Christ, who *is* this girl?" he said.

"I wish we knew," she said. She looked at him with sudden curiosity. "I thought you sprained your ankle," she said.

His smile was grim. "I did," he said. "She rubbed it and it went away."

"Oh, dear God," she said. "I don't like that at all."

"No," he stroked her hair. "I don't either." He grimaced as the thought struck him. "You went to see Charlie," he said. "How is he?"

"They can't stop the bleeding," she told him. She shuddered. "They aren't sure if he'll live."

"Good God."

"David, maybe we should go to a hotel," she said. "Get away from her."

He frowned. "It can't be *that* bad," he said. He didn't sound convinced.

"What about Val?" she asked.

"Val?"

"He was *up*. He couldn't have been more up. So was Charlie."

He didn't want to succumb to everything she said. "Honey, Val didn't remember some lines of dialogue, that's all. He didn't—"

"It was more than that and you *know* it," she countered. "He had a nervous breakdown right in front of us."

"Liz, that's carrying it a bit far. A *nervous breakdown*?"

"I'd call it that," she said. She winced. "Not to mention these goddamn headaches."

He drew in a fitful breath. "Assuming she has...certain abilities...you angered her. Did Val? Did Charlie?"

"David, who *knows* what angers her?"

He looked distressed, trying to resist the implications of what had happened. "I just can't let myself believe—" He broke off with a slight groan. "Move to a hotel?" he said. "Maybe we should move to Canada."

That brought a faint smile to her lips despite the headache. "I'll go pack," she said.

He smiled back and kissed her on the forehead. She winced and pressed her right hand to the top of her head.

"This goddamn headache," she muttered.

He looked at her with uneasy concern. "Do you...think it could have *been* her?" he asked as though he was hoping for a negative reply?

"I hate to believe it," she said, "The thought chills my blood but—" she exhaled raggedly. "It's happened too often to be a coincidence. Then there's Charlie. And Val."

He nodded, his expression one of disturbance equal to hers. All of it went counter to what he wanted to believe about the hard realities of life but he couldn't deny the facts. "I presume you've been taking your pain pills," he said, distractedly.

"Three," she answered.

"You have more?"

She shook her head, the movement causing the headache to flare. She hissed with pain.

"You're *out* of them?" he asked.

"I've had them for a long time, David," she said as though his question had been critical. "This is the first time in months—" she broke off with a faint groan, her face distorting.

"I better go get you some more," he said. "Does the prescription have a refill?"

"I think so."

He started to get up. "*David*," she said. Standing now, he looked down at her. "What?" he asked.

"I'm not sure I want to be left alone," she told him.

"She left in anger, didn't she?" he asked.

"More scared than angry," Liz replied. Her slight smile one of grim satisfaction. "I threatened to call the police," she said.

"Well, I doubt if she'll be back then," David said. "And I won't be gone more than thirty minutes."

"All right," she replied, her voice weak. "I don't want to be left alone but..." She sighed wearily. "I'm going to need those pills. I don't know how long this pain is going to last. And three pills is barely keeping a cap on it."

"I'll be as quick as I can," he told her. "Why don't you try lying down?"

"On our *bed*?" she said sarcastically.

"No, right here," he replied. "I don't know what she had in mind—especially since I wasn't here this afternoon."

"She wants your attention," Liz said. She clenched her teeth, groaning softly again. "And my absence."

"Well, it isn't going to happen," he said firmly. "She simply isn't thinking straight."

"God knows how she thinks," Liz replied.

He grunted, nodding, and moving quickly to the kitchen, he opened a cupboard drawer and took out a clean dish towel. He began to wet it at the sink. "You want to try an ice pack?" he asked.

"No," she said. "Just...go and come back as fast as you can."

"I will."

He wrung out the dish towel, started to leave the kitchen, then turned and moved to the refrigerator. Putting the dishtowel on the counter next to the refrigerator, he took a cup out of the cupboard and held it under the ice cube dispenser.

When Liz heard the noise of the ice cube maker, she called out, "No! Just *go*, David."

"Okay." He put down the cup and moved back into the living room. Liz had stretched out on the sofa, a pillow under her head. Folding the damp dish towel, he laid it across her forehead, making her twitch and open her eyes. "Thank you," she said then. "Come back as soon as you can."

"I will." He turned quickly for the bedroom, went into the bathroom and pulled open the cabinet door. The pill vial wasn't in it. He was about to call to Liz, then looked down and saw the empty prescription vial in the wastebasket.

He picked it up and dropped it in the pocket of his jacket, then returned to the living room and crossed toward the door.

"Fast," she told him.

He stopped and looked back. "Liz," he said.
"What?"

"I'd rather not ask you to do this but, if it'll help to reassure you, why don't you put the chain on the door after I leave?"

"Good idea." She started to push up, the movement making her groan again. David hurried over and assisted her to her feet, grimacing at the look of twisted pain on her face. "I'm so sorry," he said.

"It's all right," she mumbled.

He helped her across the living room and opened the door. "If you see her in the hall or outside the building, come back," she told him in a labored voice.

"I will."

"We *do* know she doesn't live in this building," she said.

"She doesn't, that was a lie," he told her.

She looked on the verge of tears again. "Jesus Christ, how many lies *did* she tell us?"

"I don't know, sweetheart," he said gently. "Just lock the door and put on the chain. I'll be right back."

"David," she said when he had almost closed the door. He looked at her. She was trying to smile despite the pain. "I believe you," she murmured.

He smiled and picked up her right hand to kiss it. "Don't worry now," he said. "We'll get through this."

He closed the door.

***

After David had left, Liz locked the door, checking and re-checking to make sure the lock was working. Then she put the chain in place. Obviously, Ganine had somehow managed to unlock the door without a key. The chain would stymie her though, she thought with grim satisfaction.

Returning to the sofa, she laid down carefully, groaning as she did. She picked up the fallen dish towel and laid it across her forehead. Like a band-aid for a fucking fractured skull, she thought, managing a tight smile.

She had barely closed her eyes when the telephone rang. "*No*," she murmured, then with a heavy sigh, reached over her head and picked up the receiver. "Yes?" she muttered.

The voice on the other end of the line was garbled, indistinct. "I'm sorry, I can't hear you," she said.

The voice was slightly clearer but still distorted. "Who *is* this?" Liz asked. In another moment I'm hanging up, she thought.

Now the voice was clearer, the garbling had been hysteria. Suddenly, she recognized the voice. "Candy?" she said.

Candy's voice was incoherent.

"Candy, slower, slower," Liz instructed her.

"It's *Val!*" Candy cried, her voice frenzied. "It's *Val!*" she repeated.

Liz felt herself shudder, feeling suddenly very cold. "What *about* him?" she asked.

"He fell apart!" Candy yelled, making Liz grimace, the pain in her head erupting again.

"What do you mean?" she said, but Candy was already interrupting her. "He screamed! He hit me! He came to pieces!"

"You don't mean *literally* he came to pieces, do you?" Liz's mind demanded. It was too insane to consider. "Where *is* he?" she asked.

"He screamed at me! He hit me and he broke things!" Candy ranted.

"Candy, where *is* he?" Liz demanded.

"He screamed and—!"

"Where *is* he, Candy?!" Liz cried, the effort making the headache flare again.

"In the hospital, the hospital!" Candy said, frantically. "The hospital! They had to put him in a straitjacket! He tried to kill them! They injected him!"

"Oh, God," Liz muttered.

She managed to get the name of the hospital from

Candy, then said, "I'll be there as soon as I can."

Candy kept speaking hysterically.

"Candy, I'll be there as soon as I can," Liz said.

She hung up on Candy's continued raving. Jesus Christ, she thought, was this Ganine again? She began to feel a sense of total helplessness. If Ganine had done such terrible things already, how much *more* could she do?

She struggled to her feet, tiny sounds of pain in her throat. Am I going to *make* it? she wondered. She had to though. Val needed her. She was sure of it.

She moved, stumbling into the kitchen and turned on the coldwater faucet in the sink. It was agony to lean over and splash water in her face. I'm not going to make it, she thought in fright. I *have* to though, she vowed. I have got to go to my brother's side. He *needs* me.

She dried her face. Oh, God, I could use some more pain pills, she thought. Well, there was no way she could wait for David to return. She moved with effort to the telephone, dialed information and asked for the number of the nearest Yellow Cab garage.

The information voice had just begun to speak the number when there was a knock on the door. She jerked her head around, crying out weakly as the pain in her head increased sharply. It couldn't be, she told herself, not so soon.

She moved haltingly to the door. "David?" she said.

"Can I come in, Mrs. Harper?" Ganine's voice asked timidly.

Before Ganine was halfway through her request Liz felt herself go rigid, the head pain beginning to pound.

"Mrs. Harper, can I come in?" Ganine sounded like a little girl pleading.

Liz couldn't speak. She had never felt so helpless in her life. Go away, a voice begged in her mind.

"I have to talk to you," Ganine said.

Liz tried to say something but couldn't make a sound.

"Mrs. Harper, *please.*" The little girl's pleading sounded pathetic now.

Suddenly, words flooded out. "*Get away from here,*" she said.

"*Please,* Mrs. Harper," Ganine said. The door handle turned. "Let me in. I have something I have to say to you."

"*Get away,*" Liz ordered in a strained voice.

"But I have to apologize." Ganine answered.

"*Get out of here,*" Liz told her.

"I can't. I have to—"

Liz cut her off, her voice abruptly rabid. "Get out of her, I said!" she cried.

"*Please,* Mrs. Harper."

Liz sobbed. "Goddamn you, *leave!*"

She backed away with a sound of dread as she heard a noise in the door lock. "No," she murmured. "*No.*"

The door lock clicked loudly and the door began to open.

"*Jesus Christ,*" Liz mumbled. It sounded like a plaintive prayer.

Her mouth fell open and she made a noise as though all breath was being sucked from her lungs.

The chain was moving by itself.

"*No,*" Liz whined. She shook her head despite the pain. This couldn't be happening.

"Why did you put on the chain?" Ganine seemed to scold her. "I only want to apologize." Liz could see her through the partially open doorway. Ganine's expression was one of distress as though Liz's use of the door chain was a cruel insult to her.

Liz's cry was like the bleating of an animal as she saw the head of the chain pop its restraint and the chain drop loose. She backed away, her face a mask of shocked fear as Ganine pushed open the door and came in. She was smiling happily. "I can do that," she said, sounding almost proud.

"*Oh, God, please go,*" Liz pleaded, a crazed edge to her voice.

"But I have to apologize to you," Ganine insisted.

Liz kept backing away from here. *Go*, was all she could think. *Go.*

"I know I shouldn't have tried to make you think I went to bed with your husband," Ganine said. "It was a stupid thing to do but I couldn't think of anything else. I just couldn't."

Liz was conscious of a terrible ambivalence in herself. On the one hand, she was being confronted by what seemed to be a timid, cringing girl begging for forgiveness. On the other hand, she was laden by a sense of dread beyond understanding.

"I need your husband's help," Ganine went on. "I'm so afraid."

"*You're* afraid?" Liz sounded almost amused. But it was a dark, body–harrowing amusement.

"I *am*," Ganine said, nodding. "And only your husband can help me."

"He *can't* help you," Liz said in a hoarse voice.

"He *can*, I *know* he can," Ganine protested.

"No, he can't!" Liz shouted, pressing both hands to her head as the pain throbbed in her head.

"What's wrong?" Ganine asked.

Liz felt herself losing control. "Please go," she mumbled.

"Are you sick?" Ganine asked in genuine concern.

"Oh, Jesus God, please go," Liz pleaded.

"Maybe I can help you," Ganine said.

Liz's voice flared suddenly, enraged. "God damn you, you're the one who did this to me!"

"I didn't do anything," Ganine said, her voice that of a child trying to appease a parent.

"*Damn you, get out of here, get out of here!*" Liz screamed.

"If you're sick, I can help you," Ganine told her.

Liz began to cry helplessly from pain and frustration. She pulled back even more as Ganine took a step toward her, a near-demented sound wavering in her throat.

"I helped your husband's ankle, I can help you too," Ganine said, smiling pleasantly.

"Oh, Jesus Christ, please—"

Ganine interrupted, her voice sounding eager now, "I helped my father when he hurt his ankle. And my mother got bad headaches all the time and I put my hand on her head and they went away."

She held out her hand. "I can help you too," she said.

Liz felt a wave of nausea in her stomach, her cheeks puffing out as though she was about to throw up.

"Don't," Ganine said.

"*What did you do to my brother?*" Liz demanded brokenly.

"I don't know your brother," Ganine answered. "I don't know what you're saying."

"For the last time." Liz's voice was guttural and shaking.

"I need your husband's help," Ganine said, a pained expression on her face. "He has to help me. He *has* to."

Something snapped in Liz's brain. Jerking around, she lunged across the living room with a staggering gait.

"What are you doing?" Ganine asked apprehensively.

Liz jerked out the bar drawer and snatched out the ice pick. She turned and lumbered toward Ganine, the ice pick brandished in her right hand. "Get out," she said, her voice barely understandable. "Get out or I'll kill you."

"No," Ganine said, backing off. "Don't hurt me. Please don't hurt me."

"Then get out, get out. *Right now.*" Liz kept moving at Ganine, her face a mask of deranged intent.

"No." Ganine said, shaking her head. "Don't hurt me. Don't you hurt me."

"Get *out*," Liz said through gritted teeth. "*Get out, you little bitch.*"

Ganine froze and closed her eyes. She flung up both her fisted hands, crossing them across her face. Her voice was shrill. "*You—can't—hurt—me!*" she cried.

Liz went rigid as the lamps began to flicker wildly, then

turn off and on in rapid succession, the room alternating rapidly between darkness and light. Suddenly, the radio went on, the sound of a Beethoven string quartet flaring up and down erratically, deafening, then cutting off, then bursting into deafening sound again. Liz's head snapped from side to side, causing the headache to flare and diminish like the music. "What are you doing?" she asked in a feeble voice, knowing that Ganine couldn't hear. "What are you *doing*?" she shouted, terrified. "*Stop* it! *Stop* it!"

The lamps went out, the room was dark. A sudden wave of cold enveloped Liz; it felt as though she'd been submerged in Artic waters. A stricken cry of dread pulsed upward in her throat; she couldn't hear it. Then, instantly, it felt to her as though an icy hand had clutched her savagely. She screamed.

It was a shriek of blinding horror.

6:47 p.m.

David was surprised to see the living room in total darkness as he entered the apartment. Reaching over to the wall switch, he flicked it up. Nothing happened. "Hell," he muttered, starting to feel his way across the room. He hissed, grimacing, as his shins collided with the coffee table. "Liz?" he called.

There was no answer. Cautiously, he made his way to the lamp beside the sofa and turned its knob. The lamp remained dark. "Oh, Christ, is it burned out?" he wondered, frowning. "Liz are you in the bedroom?" he called after reaching down to feel at the sofa.

The apartment remained still. David's expression grew concerned. "*Liz?*" he called loudly. There was no response. "What's going on?" he muttered. He shuddered. Was it possible that Ganine *had* come back while he was out? The thought caused cold alarm in his body.

He felt his way carefully to another lamp and tried to turn it on. There was no result, the room remained in total darkness.

"What the hell is going *on*?" he said. He tried not to let apprehension take control of him. Moving slowly to the kitchen, he flicked up the wall light switch. Nothing happened. "This is bad," he heard himself say. "Liz, where *are* you?!" he shouted.

There was no reply. "Dear God," he murmured, a frightened expression starting on his face.

Feeling his way to one of the kitchen drawers, he opened it and felt inside. His fingers touched the flashlight and he lifted it out, pressing forward its switch. He made a sound of relief as the beam of light appeared.

Hastily, he moved the beam around the livingroom. Liz wasn't there. Quickly, he moved to the guest bathroom and looked inside. It was empty.

"Oh, God," he mumbled, fear rising steadily in his mind. He moved to the bedroom doorway and cast the flashlight beam around the room, anxious to see Liz on the bed or in the bathroom.

The bathroom was empty and Liz was not in the bedroom. David swallowed dryly. Now I'm really worried, he thought. He felt a chilling tightness in his chest and stomach. "Liz?!" he called again, knowing that she wasn't there but unable to accept it totally. "Liz, *are you here*?!"

The apartment was deathly still. All right, he tried to reason with himself. She must have gone back to the hospital. Or Val called and she'd gone to see him. It was very unlikely, he knew. She'd been in such intense pain. She couldn't have left so soon. He wasn't gone that long.

Now what? he thought. Call Val, the hospital? He blew out a harried breath. He had no other choice. She'd gone *somewhere*, that was obvious.

When he went back into the livingroom, he saw her purse on the table by the door. The sight of it terrified him. She wouldn't leave without her purse.

Then he saw her jacket tossed across one of the chairs.

Moving swiftly to the telephone, he lifted the receiver and with a trembling finger, pressed out a number, 911.

SATURDAY

9:02 A.M.

Outside it was overcast and drizzling.

David hadn't slept all night. He still had on clothes he'd worn the day before. His face was drawn, unshaven. He'd been on the telephone so many times during the night that he'd lost count. Val—no answer after seven tries. The hospital—she wasn't there. Max and Barbara—no answer after seven attempts. The production office—far-fetched possibility; they were closed. Finally, the police. The Bureau of Missing Persons. Even Liz's mother in Ohio; a wasted, frustrating conversation, her mother losing emotional control and crying helplessly throughout the call.

He was talking to the police again, knowing that he was annoying them, that they were doing everything they could but forced to keep on checking repeatedly. Just in case, he kept telling himself. Maybe something more had developed.

"I understand," he said to the detective. "You *will* let me know if you hear anything." He was well aware that he was wasting the detective's time but couldn't help it. "Anything at all." He listened to the detective's voice. The man was remarkably patient considering how many times David had called.

After hanging up, he thought again about leaving the apartment and searching through the neighborhood. It was probably a pointless notion. Still...if it was possible that Liz had left the apartment for some reason, frightened about the possibility of Ganine returning, someone in the neighborhood might have seen her.

He scowled at himself. The police were already scouring the neighborhood, his wandering around wouldn't be a bit of use. And he had to stay by the phone. If someone called. Anyone. He groaned and rubbed his face. I need a shave, he thought. For *what*? his mind demanded irritably.

Standing, he trudged wearily into the kitchen. The only thing he'd managed to do was make himself a pot of coffee. He poured himself a cup and drank some. His stomach felt tight and acidy, he probably should stop drinking so much coffee. Or have a piece of toast, he thought. The thought was unpalatable to him.

He went back into the livingroom and slumped down on the sofa. He drank some coffee, staring at the telephone indecisively. It was a call he hadn't made. It probably was pointless. She was undoubtedly at the hospital with her husband.

Still...maybe she went home to change clothes, to do *something*. Not that she could possibly know anything about where Liz was. Still...

"Oh, God," he muttered. *Call*, he told himself. You never know. If there was any possibility at all. Putting down the cup of coffee, he pulled open the table drawer and lifted out the leather-bound telephone book, riffling through its pages until he found the number. He punched it out slowly. Be there, he thought. Know something.

When she picked up the receiver at the other end of the line, David felt a surge of hope. He knew it was irrational. But anything. *Anything.*

"Mrs. Mann?" he said.

"Yes?"

"This is David Harper, Liz Harper's husband—we met once."

"Yes?" she said again. Her tone was lifeless.

"I apologize for calling you when I know you're going through such stress about Charlie but—"

"He's dead," she said, her voice chillingly quiet.

"*What?*" He realized that she knew he'd heard because she didn't respond. "I'm so sorry," he said, a sense of guilt almost overwhelming him. "I didn't know, nobody told me. When did it happen?"

He expected her to hang up on him, his questions had been so crudely thoughtless.

She didn't hang up. "Last night," she said. "A stomach hemorrhage."

"My God," he murmured. Charlie. So hearty, so robust. *Dead?*

He knew that he should end the call but couldn't make himself do it. "I don't like asking you," he said, "but Liz has disappeared. At least it seems as though she has."

"I'm sorry," she said.

Stop! He told himself. He couldn't do it though. "Did you see her at the hospital? Has she called your apartment, left a message?"

"No, she hasn't," she said, "I'm sorry, I can't help you."

"Thank you anyway. I apologize, if I bothered you."

"That's all right."

He heard himself speaking on, even knowing it was pointless and undoubtedly distressing to her. "If her brother calls—or Max or Barbara Silver, would you ask them to phone me?"

"You can't call them?" she asked, curious and demanding at once.

"No, I haven't been able to get in touch with any of them," David said. *Get off!* his mind demanded. "Thank you, Mrs. Mann. And, once again, I'm so sorry to hear about Charlie. He was—" He broke off. *No more talk*, he ordered himself. "Goodbye," he said.

"Goodbye," she answered.

He set down the receiver and sat immobile, staring at the phone. Charlie, dead, he thought. Was it possible? That Ganine had caused the hemorrhage? The concept frightened and repelled him. But then there was Val and what had happened to him. If I could only call Ganine, he thought.

"Oh, sure, that's a *great* idea," he snarled. Jesus God! If he never saw her again, it would be too soon.

He had just slumped back on the sofa, closing his eyes, when the doorbell rang.

Oh, God, it's *her*, he thought. What was he going to do if it really was?

But maybe it was someone from the police. He tried to ignore the common-sense realization that they wouldn't come to the apartment but telephone him.

He sat, unable to move. The doorbell rang again. You have to answer it, he told himself. Even if it turns out to be Ganine.

Bracing himself, he stood and crossed the room to the door.

He started to open it, then held it back. He couldn't make himself do it without knowing. "Yes?" he said. "Who is it?"

"Emma Woodbury," the voice answered.

Woodbury, he thought. At first, it didn't register. Then he remembered. It was Ganine's last name.

But who was Emma Woodbury?

As though he'd asked the question aloud, the woman said, "I'm Ganine's mother."

Oh, God, he thought. Now what? Was *she* going to ask him to help Ganine too? He hesitated for several moments, then decided that it might prove helpful to him in understanding Ganine; at least acquiring more basic information about her.

He opened the door and looked at the short, plump, gray-haired woman standing there. Ganine looked nothing at all like her mother. She is Ganine's mother, isn't she? his mind probed suspiciously. Let that go, he ordered himself. He'd simply have to accept that she was really Ganine's mother.

"You're Doctor Harper?" the woman asked.

"Yes, I am. What can I do for you?"

The woman looked at him with an awkward expression on her face. "Is it all right if I come in?" she asked.

He wasn't sure about that. Still...the woman looked harmless enough. But then so did Ganine. David winced at the tangle of conflicting thoughts in his mind. "Yes, please do," he heard himself say. It wasn't what he really wanted but now it was done. He stepped aside and Mrs. Woodbury entered, her posture one of timid uneasiness. David closed the door and turned to her. "What can I do for you?" he repeated, then, abruptly on impulse, asked "Is this about my wife?"

The woman stared at him. "Your wife?" she said. David knew immediately that Mrs. Woodbury knew nothing about Liz. "Never mind," he told her. "What is it you want to talk about?" He already knew the answer.

"My daughter," the woman said.

He felt a chill across his body. Was Mrs. Woodbury aware of Ganine's powers?

"She isn't here, is she?" Mrs. Woodbury asked nervously.

"No," he said. "Did you think she would be?"

"I didn't know," her mother answered. "I just...wanted to make sure she wasn't here."

The chill again. David didn't know how to respond.

"Why did you ask about your wife?" Mrs. Woodbury asked. She sounded uneasy.

David felt an uncomfortable reluctance to speak about

Liz. He didn't want to ask if Ganine had mentioned Liz to her mother. What *did* they talk about? Exactly how much did Mrs. Woodbury know about her daughter?

"You aren't helping her, are you?" the woman asked abruptly.

For the third time, the chill through his body. "I...recommended another doctor," he said.

"*Don't have anything to do with her*," Mrs. Woodbury told him in a tight voice.

"*Why?*" he demanded, "What do you know about her? What kind of...powers does she have?"

Mrs. Woodbury shook her head. David couldn't tell why. Was she afraid to answer his question? Did she *know* about Ganine's powers? She had to. Why else would she be here?

"She isn't normal," Mrs. Woodbury said, "Since she was a child. She...*did* things."

"*Things?*" David was aware of how thin his voice was.

Mrs. Woodbury didn't continue, her face suddenly beset by dread. "If she knew I was here," she said. She drew in a shaking breath. "When she gets mad..."

She couldn't finish, her body wracked by a shudder.

"What *is* it?" he asked. "What does she do when she gets...angry?"

"When she was eight, she had a kitten. It scratched her hand and she..." Another indrawn, trembling breath. "She made it disappear."

"What do you mean?" he asked. "She made it disappear?" He felt a sense of total confusion and dread. He was afraid to ask any more.

"She's *evil*, Doctor," Ganine's mother said. "That's the truth of it."

He didn't know how to react. He was a doctor. Evil was an ambiguous term to him. He couldn't allow himself to take it at face value as Ganine's mother obviously did.

"What—?" he began.

"It's not her fault," Mrs. Woodbury interrupted him.

"Her father was an animal. He beat her. Abused her. Even..." She couldn't finish. "Years later," she said, "when he was coming at her to hit her again—she screamed, 'You can't hurt me!' and he fell down, his ankle twisting around. She did it to him."

Dear God, he thought.

He stiffened as she grabbed his right wrist. *"Don't try to help her,"* she told him. "No matter how she begs you. You *can't* help her. You *can't.*"

"If you don't think I can help her, why did you *come* here?" he asked.

"To warn you," she said. "To *warn* you. She'll get mad at me sometimes and, suddenly, I'll get a terrible headache."

Christalmighty, David thought. Now the headache.

"Then she'll put her hand on my head and tell me, 'Just be nice to me and the headache will go away.'"

There was a crazed look on her face now. "She killed her father when she was twelve," she said. "The doctor said it was a heart attack but there was nothing wrong with his heart, he was as strong as a bull. She made his heart stop beating. I know she did."

He couldn't speak now. He could only stare at her as she went on, her voice erratic as she spoke, up in volume, then falling to a guttural murmur. "Stay away from her," she said. "She can kill you if she wants to. There's no way to stop her. If she gets mad, she hurts people. She can kill them if she wants to. I saw her do it."

He tried to draw away from her but her clutching fingers held on rigidly. Go away, he thought. He couldn't speak though.

"We were walking one day and we passed a crippled man asking for money." She went on as though it was a litany she was compelled to finish. "Ganine felt bad about him and she said the man should die and not be in pain. After we walked past, I looked back and the man was dead. I know she did it. I'm afraid she'll kill *me* someday. She'll get mad at me and I'll die, I *know* it. I want to get away from her but I'm afraid to try. So I stay with her and clean and cook and hope she doesn't hurt me, doesn't kill me. The terrible thing about it is she's frightened by it. She doesn't know what it is and she can't control it. And she—"

She stopped and let his wrist go. "I have to go," she said. "She might come over here." She turned to leave, then twisted back. "*Stay away from her,*" she warned. "Get away somehow. *Without making her mad.* You're a doctor. You can think of something she'll believe. She's really like a child, she can be fooled. But stay away from her. If you don't, you'll never get away. I'm telling you."

She pulled open the door, crying out and recoiling at the sight of Barbara. Reacting simultaneously, Barbara caught her breath and jerked back.

Then Mrs. Woodbury shoved by her without a word and moved rapidly down the hall. Barbara watched her go in astonishment. "Who's that?" she asked.

"Ganine's mother," David told her.

She flinched at his answer. "Her *mother?*"

"Yes."

"What did she *want?*" Barbara asked.

"I'll tell you later. Come in," he told her.

She came in and David shut the door. Barbara looked pale, in an obvious state of distress. "Liz here?" she asked.

"*No.*" He looked at her worriedly. "I've been calling you since last night to ask if you knew where she was."

"You don't *know?*" she said in sudden distress.

"*No,*" he said. "I went out to get her prescription re-filled and when I got back, she was gone. I've been trying to locate her ever since."

He put his hand on her arm, her expression was stricken. "What *is* it?" he asked.

"He's dead," she told him.

"I know. The hospital called."

"The *hospital?*" she looked confused.

Oh God, he thought. We're talking about Charlie aren't we? "About Charlie," he said.

"No, dear God," she said, her voice hardly audible. *"He's dead too?"*

"What do you—?" He broke off, stunned. *"Max* is dead?"

She twitched spasmodically. "Stroke." She answered. "Last night. There wasn't time to get him to the hospital."

"Oh..." He looked at her, incredulous. *"Both* of them?" he said.

Barbara's sob broke with a terrible sound in her chest. She started crying and David put his arms around her. He wanted to ask more questions but he already knew the answers and they all added up to one thing.

Ganine.

He led her to the sofa and helped her sit. "You want a drink?" he asked.

She shook her head, dazed expression on her face. David sat beside her and put an arm around her shoulders.

"You really don't know where Liz is?" she said, still crying.

"No."

"You've called everyone?"

"Of *course.*"

Barbara began to tremble. "We have to find her," she said. "We have to get away. All of us," she said.

He stared at her, not knowing what to respond.

"You know about Val," she said.

He nodded. "We heard."

"And Candy."

"Candy?" he said. "I don't—"

"Her body's covered with a rash," she said. She made a sickened sound, "Oozing," she said. "All of it *oozing.*"

She's about to crack, he thought, or she already had.

"I came to warn you, David," Barbara said. She tried to stop crying and it made a choking noise in her throat. "We have to get away. Before it's too late." Another sobbing laugh contorted her face. "It is too late," she said. "For Max. For Charlie. For Val. For Candy. For you and me. That girl.

She's evil, David. *Evil!*"

He wanted to tell her otherwise but didn't have the strength to do it. He was a doctor, he was supposed to think in rational terms. He couldn't though. He felt submerged in a nightmare he could not control.

"Who *is* that girl?" Barbara asked in a broken, wavering voice. "Where did she come from?"

"I don't know," he answered. He felt as helpless as Barbara did.

"She killed Max—and Charlie—and maybe Val—*and where is Liz?* Is she dead too?"

"*Don't say that,*" he told her in angry resistance.

"Do you *know?*" she challenged. "She's disappeared, hasn't she?"

His shiver was spasmodic as he remembered what Ganine's mother had said about the kitten. *No*, he ordered his mind, "I'm not going to lose every bit of intellect I have."

"The other night," said Barbara in a haunted voice. "When Charlie fell down with the blood coming out of his mouth, I looked at Ganine. So did Liz. The girl looked terrified. But I could swear that she was smiling too. *Smiling*, David!"

"Barbara, take it easy," he said, knowing as he spoke, that his words were futile.

"From the moment I met her, I knew there was something wrong about her," Barbara said. "I should have said something—instead of just sitting and—" she broke off with a pitiful sob. "And arguing with Max."

"Barbara, there was nothing you could—"

"Do you know what Max and I were doing when he had the stroke?"

"Barbara—"

She ignored him. "We were fighting," she said. "*Fighting*. I was saying something awful to him. I don't remember what but it was awful. *Awful*. The last words he ever heard me say to him were *awful* words, *mean* words.

110

Oh, God forgive me!"

She began to cry again, now bitterly, her body overcome by helpless sobs. David tightened his arm around her shoulders but said nothing. There was nothing he *could* say, he realized.

Both of them jolted as though shot as the doorbell rang. "It's her," Barbara whispered, terrified.

"It might *not* be, Barbara," he tried to reassure her. "It could be someone from the police."

"No." She shook her head, staring toward the door in dread. "It's her, I know it's her."

She clutched at David's arm as he started to get up. "*Don't*," she said. "*Don't let her in.*"

"Barbara, it *could* be Liz."

She kept shaking her head. "She wouldn't ring the bell."

"She left without her key, Barbara," he said, trying to calm her.

"*No*," she insisted, her voice shaking.

The doorbell rang again and David pulled away from Barbara's clutching grip and stood. She shrank back against the sofa as he crossed the room. "No, don't," she pleaded.

David opened the door.

It *was* Ganine.

Barbara made a sound of childlike horror and pushed up clumsily. Her face a mask of resistance, she walked unevenly across the room and, without looking at Ganine, moved past her, trying not to touch her.

"Barbara?" David said.

She made no answer, hurrying down the hall. Ganine watched her leave, obviously confused by the sight. "What's wrong with her?" she asked. There was no hint of hypocrisy in her voice.

David blocked her way. "What do you want?" he asked, alarmed by shaking weakness of his voice.

"I need to talk to you," she said.

"No. No. There's nothing for us to talk about," he told her. Part of him felt fury at her, but the rest was cold apprehension. He knew now what she could do and could not dispel a feeling of anxiety about her being there.

"Please," she said, "I *have* to talk to you. I really do."

"Ganine, how can you—?" He broke off, realizing that there was no resisting it, he was afraid of her. Still…She's like a child, he remembered her mother's words. She can be fooled.

"What do you want to talk about?" He felt contemptibly weak for seeking to appease her.

"Can I come in?" she asked.

No! his voice demanded. But, already, he was stepping aside to admit her, closing the door.

"You look nervous," she said.

"I'm all right," he said, knowing instantly that he was not convincing her.

"Is it because of that woman?" she asked.

He didn't know how to answer.

"I remember her," Ganine said. "She was here Thursday night." Her expression darkened. "Did she tell you something bad about me?"

David felt himself floundering for an answer. Was it conceivable that Ganine didn't even *recall* what happened here on Thursday night, that she had no memory of it at all? Fear or no fear, he had to know.

"Do you have any idea what happened here on Thursday night?" he asked.

"Thursday night?" she said. Now the innocence in her voice sounded contrived.

"*Do* you, Ganine?" he asked.

"I don't know what you mean." It was obvious now that she was lying.

"That woman's husband died on Thursday night," he told her.

Her breath faltered. "I don't—" she started feebly.

"He had a stroke," David said. "And the man who came out of the bathroom—"

"I don't remember," she interrupted him.

"His name was Charlie Mann, my wife's executive producer—" he began.

"No, I don't—" she cut him off.

"He died yesterday morning," he told her."He had an internal hemorrhage. I told you about him yesterday."

"No." She shook her head, looking frightened.

"And my wife's brother had a nervous breakdown. It started Thursday night when he was trying to deliver a speech."

"*I don't remember,*" she said. She sounded irritated now.

Her change of mood alarmed him but he couldn't stop himself. "His girlfriend—you remember, her name is Candy—has a rash all over her body with running sores."

"*I don't know anything about it,*" she insisted.

"And my wife is gone," he said. "She's *disappeared.*" He tried to make her think about what she'd done to her kitten.

"I don't know anything about your wife," she said. "I don't know anything about your friends."

"Where *is* she, Ganine?" he asked. He knew he was risking his life but couldn't stop himself now. He had to know.

"*I don't know what you mean,*" she said. Her anger was apparent. The sight of it chilled him but he wouldn't back down now. He had to *know.*

"I think you do," he said.

She shuddered. "No, I don't," she said. She sounded frightened but it didn't lessen his dread. He believed totally now what she was capable of doing.

He braced himself. "You're lying, Ganine," he said.

She shook her head. "No," she insisted. "I don't know anything."

"You're lying."

"*I don't lie.*" Her tense expression terrified him. He was amazed at himself for pressing on. "Where's my wife?" he asked.

"*I don't know,*" she said.

"I think you do."

She stared at him, breath quickening. Suddenly, she turned to leave. "All right, don't help me," she said. "I can—"

She broke off with a gasp of surprise as David lunged to block her way. "*You aren't leaving,*" he told her. You're committing suicide! his mind cried.

"Yes, I am," she said.

"*No.*" He pushed her back and she retreated, her expression hardening to one of disbelief. "Don't hurt me," she said.

"*Hurt* you?" he answered. "Everyone who's come in contact with you since Thursday night has been hurt." He stiffened. "Hurt," he said. "*Destroyed.*"

"I have to go home," she told him, sounding like a frightened child.

"*To your mother?*" he snapped. "So you can hurt *her?*"

She looked startled. "My *mother?*" she asked.

"She was here," he said, feeling guilty for betraying her mother but unable to contain his rage. "She told me all about you," he said. "About your father."

She tried to pull open the door but David stopped her. "You're not going," he told her, grabbing her wrist.

She made a sound like the whimpering of a dog. "Don't hurt me," she begged.

"*Damn* you," he muttered.

"Please let go of me," she said.

"*Where's my wife?!*" he shouted.

Jerking free, she backed away, glaring at him in fury.

"All right!" she cried. "You want to know where she is?!"

David felt his body going rigid. *Don't,* he thought.

"*You want to know where she is?!*" she cried again. "All right! *All right!*"

Whirling, she pointed at a section of the wall. "There!" she raged. "*There!*"

David glanced at the wall, then back at Ganine. Had she lost her mind?

"*Just like my kitten!*" she cried.

David looked back at the wall, started to turn to Ganine again, then jerked his head around, staring at the wall, his eyes widening as he saw what was happening. He felt his stomach muscles drawing in. He couldn't seem to breathe.

The wall was very slowly bulging outward. Flakes of paint began to drizzle off. Then the plaster started cracking, pieces of it crumbling loose and falling to the floor. No, he thought, mindlessly. No. Oh, no.

A larger piece of plaster dropped to the floor now and David sucked in horror-stricken breath of what he saw.

A plaster-whitened hand.

Suddenly, it seemed to him as though his heart had stopped and breath was unavailable to him. His face a frozen mask, he gaped at the crumbling wall as chunks of plaster continued to drop from it.

Ganine shrieked. "*There's* your wife!"

His mouth fell open as he saw, in the wall, an arm, a section of hip. He made a sickened noise as a big piece of plaster fell away from Liz's white, staring face. He couldn't move or think, standing, frozen, as the toppling fragments revealed Liz's corpse powdered with plaster dust. David heard a feeble whining sound in his throat.

Then Ganine made it worse.

"You want your precious wife?!" she screamed. "He *wants* you now! Your husband *wants* you, Mrs. Harper!"

David made a choking sound of shock as Liz began to move. *No*, he thought. It was the only word his harrowed mind could manage.

He wanted to move, to turn, to flee as Liz's corpse broke out from the remaining section of wall and started toward him with a shuffling stiffness. David felt a wave of icy dread envelope him as her right arm slowly, jerkingly, rose.

She still held the ice pick in her hand.

David backed away unconsciously, staring at her, dazed and unbelieving, as she kept advancing toward him, her movements jerking and mechanical. He heard his voice begin to plead. "No. No."

He backed into the coffee table, lost his equilibrium and fell back thrashingly. With a stricken cry, he struggled to his feet. "Make it stop," he begged, his voice just audible.

"No!" Ganine cried, smiling fiercely, glaring with avenging fury.

"Make it stop!" he screamed, his face rigid with maddened horror.

"No!" she cried. "I *won't!*"

David backed off further, one arm raised to block the ice pick stab. Liz's corpse was almost to him now. Her arm hitched higher, brandishing the pick, her lifeless face without expression.

David screamed in mindless terror.

He started violently as Liz was yanked back by some invisible force and flung to the floor like a rag doll. At the same instant, Ganine cried out in shock, then stood with stunned disability. David looked at her, paralyzed with amazement, then looked down at Liz's corpse sprawled motionless on the floor.

His gaze jumped back to Ganine as she began to speak. But it was not Ganine's voice. Where hers had been timid and fearful or childishly demented, this voice—deeper than hers—spoke with absolute authority.

"You will have to forgive her," the voice told David. "She is a sick, unknowing child who has no conception whatsoever as to what has happened to her."

David felt his terror turn to awe as he listened to the continuing voice.

"It was assumed, mistakenly, that she could maintain her separate existence unimpeded. That enough awareness of the self which had assimilated her would filter down into her consciousness. It was obviously not so. She is disordered, her bestowed power utilized too randomly, creating violence. She has become too lethal and must be restrained. It is unfortunate that she was chosen to be one of the first. It was an errant choice although she seemed to possess the necessary qualifications."

David's voice was dazed. "Who—?" he started.

"—am I?" the voice broke in imperiously.

The voice was still then. David began to speak, then sensed that he had to wait, that somehow, he was forbidden to interrogate.

The voice spoke once again.

"You are permitted to be told, because of your wife," it said. It was, quite clearly, he now realized, a woman's voice. But not Ganine's. Although Ganine's face looked at him with an expression of detached assurance, he knew it wasn't she who spoke to him.

"Men and women can no longer co-exist," the woman said, her tone malignant but controlled. "We are sundered beings.

"There is only one Earth," she continued. "Only one force can control it. This was not inevitable at the beginning but now is so.

"Nature can no longer be a conquest. No longer will you be empowered to desolate its very existence. From this day forth, you will not despoil its growth. You will, no more, infect its lakes and rivers and its oceans. You will, no longer, fill its atmosphere with wasting poisons.

"You will, no longer, butcher seals and whales and dolphins or any other rightful creature in the seas. You will, no longer, slaughter animals for greed or sport.

"No longer will your gender be given leave to turn its back on all responsibility to age, to race or to religious faith. You will ignore, no further, what is ancient, debase, no further, what is different. You have abused your last human being, raped your last human being, gassed and burned and blown to bloody shreds your last human being. Politics and power blight existence. You will not be privileged to blight existence any longer.

"Your betrayal of me now also ceases. I will not be brutalized again. I am not an object, not a slave, neither inferior nor invalid. I am awareness and compassion. I do not destroy but create. I do not deform but sustain. I have lived forever. I will always live.

"I am Woman."

Whatever held Ganine in domination gazed silently at David for several moments, then turned toward the door.

"*Wait*," David said.

The woman in Ganine turned back to look at him.

"*There has to be an answer.*"

"The answer is already taking place," the woman's voice informed him. "The child within this instrument is unsired by man. It will be female. In due time, all newborn babies will be female. Male infants will abort or die at birth. The race, unsullied by the male distraction, will endure. Conception will be dealt with in another way.

"Women will control the Earth.

"Not those women who have defiled themselves to satisfy the male. Not those who have attempted to corrupt their gender by becoming males themselves in any way. Not those who fail to understand the natural purpose of our Being. These, too, shall perish. Your wife might have been one of these."

"But surely—" he protested.

The voice ignored him. "What will remain will be a permutation," she continued. "Nature altered by nature to undo the eons of offense. What will remain will be a new vitality, a new substance. Gradually, a perfect woman will emerge. A transcendent force of life dedicated to—"

The voice broke off, then told him, "You have heard enough and you will not repeat it."

Ganine—the woman—looked at him with pity.

"It is unfortunate," she said. "There might have been a chance with such as you.

"*Now it is too late.*"

She turned and left the apartment, leaving the door open. David stared toward the hallway, feeling lost and impotent.

In his chest, his heart beat slowly, labouredly.

MONDAY

STATION **KBNY**, 3:01 P.M. Doctor David Harper. *Candidly speaking.*

I am not going to answer questions today. Instead, I am going to speak to you about a subject we've discussed for several weeks now, namely the feminist movement. I've said that I think it's failing and I still believe that. I was referring to its social aspect though, as a revolution, it cannot succeed.

But there is, also, *evolution.*

The human fetus is, by nature, initially female. It becomes male if the genetic code determines it. But, first, it is female.

The oldest known representation of the Deity is the figure of a woman. Nature and its secrets have always been associated with women. Worship of the moon, in ancient times, was worship of creative power in the female — of her attunement with natural law.

Because this law has been and is being broken, the disenchantment goes beyond the demands of feminism. It gravitates into the area of total life upon the environment of this planet. A planet on which women live but have had no real voice.

Until now.

Social justice cannot be achieved while man is dominant. Accordingly, the same genetic code which turns a female fetus into a male must, of necessity, be re-oriented.

Let me quote from Esther Harding.

"Even today, they say, certain babies are begotten by the Moon, not by any mortal father. Such children are marked out for some great destiny as befits their celestial parentage."

Concluding then...

A poem from the sixth century reads as follows:

Lady of Ladies, Goddess of Goddesses
Queen of all peoples, Directress of mankind
Thou art great, thou art exalted
All mankind boweth down before thy power
Look upon me, O my Lady and accept
                              my supplication
Cry unto me "It is enough!" and let thy
                    spirit be appeased.

This spirit is *being* appeased. There is, upon this Earth, as I now speak to you, a *new* woman. Who carries, in her womb, the embryo of what is soon to be—*oh, no.* Listen to me. What is happening is in its infancy. It can be prevented if we— I'm having trouble breathing. *Oh!* Dear God, my *chest!* The *pain.* I'm *choking.* Listen! This is *happening!* We must—oh, dear *God!*

Turn it off! Right now!

I can't! It won't go off!

Jesus Christ, what's happening?!

Call an ambulance! He's having a goddamn heart attack!

For Chrissake, *turn the mike off!*

Ladies and gentlemen—*Please stand by.*